The Beacon

The Crystal Coast Series

The
Beacon

Chrissy Lessey

Tenacious Books Publishing

Published by Tenacious Books Publishing

Published in 2017 by Tenacious Books Publishing
tenaciousbooks@gmail.com

This book is a work of fiction. Names, characters, places, and incidents are either the product of the author's imagination or are used fictitiously.

Library of Congress Cataloging-in-Publication Data
The Beacon/ Chrissy Lessey
ISBN 978-0-9989518-4-3 (e-book)
ISBN 978-0-9989518-5-0 (print)

Cover Image: © iStock
Cover Design: Anita B. Carroll www.race-point.com
Book Design: Erin Rhew www.erinrhewbooks.com

Printed in the United States of America

www.tenaciousbookspublishing.com

For Katherine

prologue

September 1745

Lucia sat alone at her table with a crow quill poised in her wrinkled hand. A heavy, leather-bound book lay open before her. She had stayed up all night, reviewing and amending its contents by the steady flame of a single candle. Now, as the first of the sun's rays began to poke through the windows, she knew she must hurry to complete her work. Beth would arrive soon.

In spite of the decades she'd spent compiling the book, her mind still raced with unwritten revelations from the amulet, memories of her own time, and visions of a future yet to come. It had been impossible to record every detail, but she'd done her best to be thorough. The spells and history she'd included would be a poor substitute for the knowledge contained within the amethyst. She could only hope it would be sufficient. The success of the next leader depended on it.

Leader. When Lucia passed the amulet to her daughter, Charlotte, she had relinquished the appellation of queen without hesitation and adopted the title of leader for herself. It didn't matter how her people addressed her. She knew she had their respect.

She stared through the window, seeing nothing and everything at once. By now, her grandchildren would be grown. Perhaps they'd already started their own families. She sighed. The line had continued without her. But then again, that had been the plan all along. Though her heart ached daily over Charlotte's absence, Lucia found comfort in the knowledge that her decision had led to lasting safety for her kind.

She had bought her people a measure of freedom with the coin of her own sacrifice.

She shivered and glanced at her great stone hearth. For once, no fire burned within its blackened interior. Though she missed the symphony of pops and cracks that came from dancing flames, she had spared herself the trouble of building a fire. The rising sun would warm the cottage soon enough, and she had no need to cook on this day. She returned her attention to her work.

Lucia's fingers trembled with age and frailty as she dipped her quill into the pewter inkwell. She needed to add one last note to the book so her successors could share the benefit of her visions.

I have seen a wondrous future for our people, one predicated on the choice I made years ago. You must resist the desire to connect with the other witches in Beaufort. You and your descendants will enjoy lasting safety, but only if you remain separate from Charlotte's group. This is how it is in my visions. This is how you must live to ensure safety for all.

Sunlight poured through the windows now, bathing the cottage in its glow. Lucia placed her quill on the table and extinguished the candle. She could no longer deny the exhaustion that had crept into her body.

Lucia had prepared for this inevitable day ever since she led her people from their island home to a new settlement on the North Carolina coast. Here, her group had thrived as the port town known as Wilmington flourished around them. They'd succeeded in keeping their magic a secret, even as a new generation of witches grew up among the diverse settlers who also lived in their community. Since they'd managed that, she had no doubt they could weather the changes to come.

A soft knock tapped at her door.

She did not move from her chair. "Come in." The weakness in her voice came as no surprise. Her strength had been waning for a long while.

Beth bustled into the cottage and closed the door behind her. Her silky black braid swept across her back as she twirled around to face Lucia. Though she was a young woman, wrinkles of worry deepened across her forehead when she took in the sight of her mentor.

"How are you feeling today?" Beth settled into a chair at the table.

"Exactly how I expected to feel." Lucia gave a thin smile. "What about you? Are you ready?"

Beth peered down at the open book and bit her lip. "I still worry that I'm not strong enough. My concern grows ever greater as we near..." She blinked and fell silent for a moment before speaking again. "Wouldn't a pure-blooded witch be a more appropriate successor?"

Lucia tucked a lock of white hair behind her ear as she considered Beth's question. The young woman was the product of a union between a witch and a native man who had remained in the area when his tribe moved north. In the years since their arrival, it had become common practice for the witches to marry people outside of their group. Sometimes, the children produced from those unions went on to develop powerful magic. Other times, the magic in the offspring was limited or non-existent. But this fact did not bother Lucia. Her visions had revealed a long future of witches living side by side with those who did not share their gift. In Beth, she saw an opportunity.

"Beth, you represent our future. You are living proof that we can not only exist among the others, but we can live in harmony with them." Lucia patted her hand. "Your magical talents are more than sufficient for the task ahead. I wouldn't have chosen you otherwise."

Beth traced her finger along the edge of the table. "Are you sure the others will accept me as their leader?"

"I have already taken care of that." Lucia gave a slight nod. "I've said time and again that you are my chosen successor. Besides, they all know you have trained with me since you were a little girl. Acceptance will not be an issue. What you need to be concerned with is how you will earn—and keep—their respect."

"I have a plan for that actually." A flash of sly confidence chased the doubt from Beth's expression, and she grinned.

Lucia arched an eyebrow. "I would love to hear it."

Beth stood and smoothed her skirt before stepping in front of the stone hearth. She beamed with excitement as she caught Lucia's eye. "Watch me."

"I'm watching." Lucia kept her focus fixed on the young witch, whose image faded until no trace of her remained.

Beth had vanished.

Lucia blinked. Given her gift of foresight, she was seldom surprised, so she couldn't help but relish the novelty of the experience. If she'd had the strength, she would have crept closer to investigate Beth's disappearance. Instead, she stared at the empty space from her seat at the table. A few witches had the ability to travel in an instant, disappearing from one location only to reappear in another. However, this magic was different. Lucia sensed that Beth remained nearby. "Where are you?"

"I'm still here." Her reply came from the area in front of the hearth, but there was no sign of the young witch.

"Show yourself so we can discuss your plan."

Beth reappeared as swiftly as she had disappeared. She extended her arms in a display of proud showmanship. "What do you think?"

"It's a clever trick. I've used similar magic myself." Lucia thought of the amulet and raised her hand to the spot on her chest where it once resided. Witch queens throughout history had made the necklace invisible in order to hide it from outsiders. "But I've never seen anyone successfully conceal an *entire* person before. Tell me how you did it—and how this affects our people."

"Well…I've been practicing for several months. Now I can do this on a much larger scale." She ran her hand across the rough stone surface of the hearth. "You see, I drew on the natural energy of the stones. I pulled their likeness over me like a cloak until I was no longer visible to you."

"That's a clever approach." Lucia nodded in approval. "*Very* impressive magic."

Eyes gleaming, Beth propped her hands on her hips. "Now, imagine drawing on the power of the ocean. We could disguise just about anything on the open water."

Lucia sighed and sank back in her chair. She sensed what would come next.

"We could return to our island! I could hide it easily." Beth's words tumbled out too fast. "I can even teach the others how to do it. We wouldn't have to worry about pirates, or anyone else, discovering our magic. We can be truly free once again!"

"Come here, my dear." Lucia spoke with tenderness as she reached for Beth's hand. "I'm sure you've heard about how wonderful our time on the island was. It's all true. However, you cannot take our people back there. Not ever." She gestured toward the open book. "I have seen centuries of peace for our group, as well as Charlotte's. In each of those visions, we remain in Wilmington, and my daughter's group stays in Beaufort. For that future to come to pass, we must stay here."

Beth opened her mouth as if to speak but silenced herself before uttering a word. Her dejected gaze dropped to the wooden floor. "I understand." Her shoulders slumped as she returned to her chair at the table.

"I sincerely hope you do." Lucia's voice had grown even weaker, but she pressed on. "This is an important skill. Certainly, it's one that you should teach the others. You never know when this magic might become useful."

Beth's frown began to fade. "I'll do that."

"There's something else."

"Yes?"

"I know you put a great deal of effort into mastering that cloaking magic." Lucia gave her the broadest smile she could muster in her feeble state. "I am *proud* of you."

"Thank you." Beth heaved a great sigh and raised her chin as the remaining traces of her disappointment evaporated.

Lucia clasped her hands together, pleased with the young witch's reaction to her praise. Soon, their people would look to Beth for the same sort of validation. In the long years to come,

Lucia hoped her protégé would remember how it felt to receive the leader's approval.

"Have you had your morning meal yet?" Beth rose from her chair. "I would be happy to prepare something for you."

"Please don't trouble yourself. I have no appetite." Lucia waved her hand, dismissing the idea. "In fact, I need to rest now. Will you help me to my bed?"

"Of course." Beth wrapped her arm around Lucia's waist and extended her hand for additional support while the former queen stood from her seat at the table.

Lucia's feet shuffled across the floorboards as she inched toward her bed. Without warning, she stopped in her tracks. "My dear, I nearly forgot! You'll need to leave a basket by your door in the morning. Also, add a note about it in the book so the tradition will continue through the generations."

"The basket used to hold offerings for the new queen?" Beth's brow furrowed in confusion.

"There can only be one queen, and that is Charlotte." Lucia stepped forward once more, gripping Beth's hand for support. "This basket will be used to receive gifts welcoming the new *leader*."

Beth sucked in a sharp breath and straightened her back. "You said I'll need the basket in the morning. Are you saying you won't survive the night?"

"My dear, I won't survive another hour."

The young witch gasped. "There must be something I can do!"

Lucia only shook her head.

Beth fell silent as they continued across the room. She helped Lucia lay down and then covered her with a thick quilt.

Lucia welcomed the comfort of her bed. Overcome with exhaustion, there was nowhere else she wanted to be.

"I thought we had more time…" Beth wiped a tear from her smooth cheek.

"This is as it should be. I am ready, and so are you." Lucia let her eyes close, though she remained awake. "I'm going to join all the witches who came before me. They wait for me now on the other side of the veil. My mother will be there, and someday, Charlotte will join us too. I look forward to it actually."

She sensed Beth's presence at her side as she prepared to let herself slip away. She had no more work to do. The tension in her body dissipated, and her racing thoughts settled as serenity washed over her. It wouldn't be long now.

Unbidden, a terrifying vision flashed in her mind, forcing her to witness a distant future. Chilling images made themselves known. A queen murdered in front of her coven. A precious little boy in peril. The amulet in the hands of unfettered evil.

Her face pinched in agony. The darkest witch her people had ever known would rise and call herself their queen.

"Lucia! What is it? Are you in pain?" Beth grasped her hand. "How can I help?"

Lucia's eyes sprung open, wide with terror. "Heed the call of the Diamond Lady!" Beads of sweat formed on her brow as her breaths came faster. "Write it in the book. Do it now so you won't forget!"

She closed her eyes once more.

"Who is the Diamond Lady?"

Beth's voice sounded so very far away.

Chapter one

Stevie

In the early morning hours, Stevie Lewis crept through her front door with the stealth of a hungry cat. Coffee mug in hand, she stepped out onto her porch and pulled the heavy door behind her, holding her breath as it clicked closed. Satisfied that she'd made her escape without detection, she let out a sigh worthy of both her relief and frustration.

Too much hassle just to steal a few moments of solitude.

Her foot brushed the basket that Alice had placed by her door. It now contained several new offerings of handmade soaps, candles, gemstones, and teas. The Beaufort witches had been generous in honoring her as their new queen, but she decided to look over the gifts later. For now, she was grateful to have a little time to herself.

Since her mother's death four days earlier, the coven had rallied around her, even as she wavered in her decision to accept her new role as their queen. Stevie was certain that they had worked out a schedule among themselves to ensure she'd never have a moment alone. She reminded herself that they only wanted to protect her, not just from her grief but also from Susan's next attack.

But they can't save me from either one.

Stevie shook her head in a futile attempt to banish the dire thoughts and then wrapped her hands around her mug, warming them. It helped stave off the chill of the October morning, but it did nothing to soothe the grief that had become her constant companion.

In search of a distraction, she glanced to the east and marveled at the sight before her. The night sky bled bold shades of red as the sun sliced its way through the darkness. A new day had dawned.

Stevie filled her lungs with crisp salt air and shifted her focus across the street to the calm water of Taylor's Creek. The low hum of a fishing boat's motor grew louder as it passed by on its way through the inlet. Birds chirped from their hidden roosts in the surrounding trees. A skinny yellow lab, probably a stray, meandered down the sidewalk. The dog stopped at Stevie's gate and stared at her for a moment before continuing down Front Street.

She had watched the town of Beaufort gently awaken on more occasions than she could count, but this time was different. It was the first morning since she'd officially accepted her birthright as queen and, in doing so, had declared war on the murderous dark witch who'd stolen the amulet.

Stevie's chest tightened as she recalled Susan's ominous words. *There can only be one queen.*

But now there were two—one by birth and one by theft.

It was only a matter of time before the dark witch came for her.

She had no intention of waiting for Susan to make her next move. With the responsibility of the coven's safety on her shoulders, Stevie had no choice but to take action soon.

More than once since her mother's death, she'd given serious thought to taking Charlie and running as far away from Beaufort as she could get. However, she knew that was nothing more than idle fantasy. She and Charlie were the last remaining direct descendants of Lucia, and Stevie was the only one who could challenge Susan's false claim to the amulet.

Besides, Susan would come for her no matter where she sought refuge.

The dark witch's evil knew no bounds. Between her own incredible magic and the power supplied by the stolen amulet, Susan had already proven herself stronger than the combined efforts of the coven members. She could appear at any moment and cut Stevie down, just as she had done to Patricia. She might choose to go after Charlie as well. Stevie's jaw clenched at the thought.

The door creaked open behind her, but she did not turn to see who had come to rescue her from her solitary ruminations. She already knew.

Dylan slipped his arms around her waist. "Why don't you lower your mental shield? Let me take on some of those worries for you."

Stevie let herself relax against his broad chest. Dylan Kent hadn't left her side since her mother's death. She was tempted to let him read her mind. However, she'd been keeping a secret from him, one he would no doubt discover if she let him in while her thoughts were so unfocused.

Soon, she would have to tell him about Vanessa's return, but not now. The coven had been through so much already. She couldn't bring herself to add more to his burden.

Another dog, this one small and fluffy, pranced down the sidewalk on the far side of the street. It stopped in front of

Stevie's house, sniffing the air fervently as though it sought a specific scent. Satisfied by whatever it had or had not detected, it wagged its tail and then continued down the street.

"That's the second dog I've seen this morning." Stevie took another sip of her coffee.

"There are probably many more nearby that you haven't seen yet. Ruth has all of the strays guarding the house." Dylan lowered his arms and stood next to Stevie. Then he leaned over the porch railing and peered into the bushes below. "There's another one down there." He pointed to an old beagle lying under the low green canopy.

"You're kidding! What exactly will these dogs do when Susan comes for me?"

"Ruth says they'll let us know if you're in danger."

"A lot of good that will do." She shook her head.

"I know it's a stretch, but it's better than nothing." Dylan stroked her arm as if to reassure her. "Have you noticed the line of sea salt around the house?"

She tilted her head and then glanced back at her house. Her gaze drifted down to the wooden boards of the porch, where she spotted the grains of salt standing sentinel along the outer perimeter of her historic home. The line grew thicker in front of the door and the windows, providing additional protection at points of entry.

"Let me guess." Stevie touched her finger to her chin. "This was Lexi's doing."

Dylan nodded. "That's right. It's to keep evil from entering the house."

She propped her hand on her hip. "Do you really think a line of salt can keep Susan at bay?"

"We're all just doing everything we can to keep you safe."

"I think you've all taken this 'queen' stuff a little too far." Stevie pursed her lips. "You are *not* my guards."

"I don't protect you because you're my queen. I protect you because you're my Stevie." He leaned in and planted a kiss on her forehead.

She sighed. As queen, it was her responsibility to protect him, but she still had no idea how to do it.

"My new boat will be delivered today." Dylan eyed his empty dock on the other side of the street. "Maybe we can go for a ride later. It'll help you relax."

Stevie cringed. She'd been responsible for blowing up the first one when Vanessa had tried to use it to escape. "I'm sorry I destroyed your boat."

"I'm not!" Dylan grinned. "You did what you had to do to save yourself and Charlie. And you eliminated Vanessa in the process. Can you imagine how much trouble we'd all be in if we had to fight her as well as her mother?"

Stevie did not reply. Instead, she swallowed hard and once again turned eastward. Just a few blocks away, a luxurious yacht sat moored at the town dock. That boat was home to the greatest threats her family had ever encountered.

Susan *and* Vanessa.

Chapter two

Vanessa

Vanessa Moore woke to the sound of ice clinking against glass. She had a vague recollection of drifting off to sleep on the leather couch the night before. Now, as the stiffness in her neck made itself known, she regretted her decision to stay there instead of retiring to her private room.

She opened her eyes and listened to her mother open and slam shut cabinet doors in the yacht's galley. Creating a storm of avoidable clatter and growled curses, the older witch made no effort to keep the noise down, in spite of the fact that her daughter had been sleeping soundly just a few feet away in the living area. If anything, Vanessa suspected that Susan was trying to wake her on purpose.

Vanessa rose from the couch, her movements jostling the delicate, newly formed skin on her face and arm. She stifled a groan. Her burns always hurt more first thing in the morning.

Clutching a fresh Bloody Mary in her bony hand, Susan walked over to the well-stocked bar to top off the concoction with a considerable dose of vodka. She slipped a fresh celery stalk into her glass. "Fix yourself a drink and join me on the deck. We have some celebrating to do." It was not a suggestion.

"It's a little early for me." Vanessa didn't look at her mother. She made her way to the coffee maker instead, relieved that she had remembered to set its timer the night before. Not long ago, she could have acquired a hot cup of coffee with little more than a thought. Now, with her powers bound by the coven, she had no choice but to pour herself a cup the old-fashioned way.

Susan stepped closer to Vanessa, narrowing her eyes. "You don't seem very excited about me being the new queen."

Vanessa had only been awake for a few minutes and already her mother was attempting to pick a fight. She rested her coffee mug on the countertop. "I guess I just don't see the point in all of this. You have declared yourself queen of a fraction of a small town's population. To what end?" She nodded to the smooth, pear-shaped amethyst that dangled from the gold chain around her mother's neck. "You could go anywhere and do anything you want with that kind of power."

Vanessa regretted her words as soon as she'd said them. She knew better than to question Susan's motives, even if they were irrational. She raised her coffee mug to her lips as the weight of her mother's glare bore down on her.

"This is a matter of principle!" Susan drained her drink and then deposited her glass on the counter with an unnerving thump.

Vanessa didn't want to fuel Susan's growing rage, but she knew her mother would not just let the conversation drop. "But most of the witches in town don't even know about the amulet, much less that you have it."

"Oh, I intend to fix that." Susan gripped the pendant. "With this, I have access to all of the knowledge possessed by the queens who came before me. Our people placed them all on pedestals simply because of their bloodline, but they were *not* special. Most weren't even as powerful as I am. How is that fair?" Susan began to pace across the length of the main cabin. "What about me?"

Vanessa sipped her coffee as she watched her mother's tirade gain momentum. The day had only just begun, and yet, she already knew it would be long one.

"I'm a direct descendant of Blackbeard! Shouldn't that count for something?" Susan extended her arms as if to seek validation for her claim.

Vanessa saw no point in arguing with her. There wasn't any chance her mother would find error in her own wayward logic. She hoped Susan's growing rage would burn out on its own soon.

"It seems the coven members have kept the circumstances surrounding Patricia's death a secret. I've heard no rumblings among the local witches." Susan continued to pace. "So no one knows I'm the one who put an end to her reign. Now they assume Stevie is their new queen."

Susan grabbed the tomato juice from the refrigerator and began to prepare herself another Bloody Mary. Vanessa wondered why her mother didn't use her magic to make her drinks. Perhaps she enjoyed the ritual of making them by hand, or maybe she was too angry to focus her magic on the task. Whatever the case, she wasn't curious enough to ask.

Having completed her preparations, Susan stirred her drink with the celery stalk. "I guess I'll just have to kill Stevie and the boy next. Then there will be no one left of Lucia's line."

Coffee sloshed out of Vanessa's mug as an unexpected tremble overtook her. She stole a quick glimpse of Susan, who was now absorbed in guzzling her second breakfast libation. Vanessa tried and failed to steady her hand.

Without a word, she returned her mug to the counter. Susan had her attention now.

Chapter three

Stevie

S tevie held five-year-old Charlie's hand as they walked to her parents' cottage on Friday afternoon. She wanted to enjoy the time alone with her son. Instead, she watched for potential dangers with every step. They passed one white picket fence after another as well as tidy rows of southern live oaks—the same scenery they'd walked by countless times before. At first glance, it all *seemed* safe. But she no longer trusted what she saw with her own eyes. Susan's attacks on her family had left scars too deep to heal.

She stifled a shudder, recalling the dark witch's elaborate illusion designed to convince the coven that the entire town of Beaufort had turned on them. Between the witch hunt hallucinations and Susan's knack for flawless magical disguises, the coven had almost fled their beloved hometown. Discovering that their gifts had remained a secret from their non-witch neighbors should have come as happy news. But it didn't. Stevie could find no joy after the loss she'd endured.

She bristled as she spotted one of her mother's neighbors pulling weeds from his garden. He might be an innocent man. Or he might be Susan in disguise. Stevie couldn't tell the difference.

She peered down at Charlie to see if he had any reaction to the man. Immune to Susan's forced hallucinations and disguises, he'd become a critical component in the coven's magical security system. Whether this was due to his autism or simply the result of an unusual magical gift, Stevie didn't know. Whatever the case, his immunity would spare him the torment of Susan's mind games. But it couldn't save him from anything else she might try.

Charlie's gaze flicked to the gardener and then back down to the sidewalk. He showed no fear. They were safe. For now.

Stevie exhaled a slow breath but remained vigilant. They might not be so lucky the next time.

She wanted to honor the peaceful nature of her people and avoid violence, but the coven couldn't bind Susan's magic while she was in possession of the amethyst. Stevie would have to retrieve the amulet from the formidable witch, or she'd have to kill her. But so far, she hadn't come up with a workable plan for either option.

Charlie tugged on her hand, pulling her away from her worries. He pointed to a yellow lab that walked on the opposite side of the street. "Magic."

In spite of her tension, Stevie smiled when Charlie spoke. *Magic* was the only word he'd said aloud since he was two years old. Every time he said it, she remembered how far he had come since he received his autism diagnosis. Not long ago, she'd thought Charlie would never speak again. Now, she awaited new additions to his vocabulary. Hope was the most potent magic she had ever known.

"That's right, Charlie. I think I saw that same dog early this morning. Ruth sent the strays to watch out for us." Maybe he'd take comfort in that, even if Stevie didn't.

They reached the small cottage that had once been her childhood home. She gave a quick knock and then opened the front door.

She stepped into the foyer. "Dad? It's just us."

"Come on in, Stephanie. I'm in the den." His call came from the back of the house.

Half expecting the chords of an old Fleetwood Mac song to greet her, Stevie froze in the doorway, jarred by the quiet stillness of the house. No music. No off-key singing came from the kitchen. Her mother wouldn't round the corner and welcome her with a hug. There would be no more lectures or unsolicited advice.

The emptiness left in the wake of her mother's death surrounded her. *She's gone.* Stevie blinked as a thick lump formed in her throat. For her father's sake, she took a moment to compose herself before proceeding to the den.

Stevie found her dad reclined in his favorite chair, facing the television he had not turned on. She wondered how long he had been sitting there in silence.

"Hey, Dad." She bent down to give him a quick hug. Then she stepped back to make room for Charlie to embrace his grandfather.

Stevie studied her father's weary expression. Drawn by grief and exhaustion, deep wrinkles creased his brow, and the bags under his bloodshot eyes broadcast his lack of sleep. "We just wanted to check in on you. Do you need help with anything around here? Can I make dinner for you?"

"Please, don't make any more food." Jim raised his hand in protest. "Alice and the neighbors have been bringing meals every day since…" He let out a ragged sigh. "Take some of it home with you. I'll never get through it all."

Charlie walked over to the toy bin Patricia had kept for him in the corner, and Stevie took a seat on the couch.

She resisted the urge to ask her father how he was doing, a ridiculous question to ask right now anyway. He wasn't okay, and neither was she. She couldn't help but wonder if they would ever be *okay* again.

"All right. No food." She rubbed her hands together and glanced around the room in search of something to do. "What about laundry? I can get you caught up on that."

"You're determined to help in some way, aren't you?"

Stevie nodded.

"You're just like your mother." The slightest hint of a smile tugged at the corner of his mouth as he returned his gaze to the blank television screen.

"I hope so." Stevie bit down on her quivering lip.

She wished she could tell her father the truth about her mother. She wanted him to know that Patricia had been a great queen, descended from a long line of powerful witches. He had no idea that his wife had been a hero who sacrificed her life defending her people from evil.

But Stevie could never say these things to him. As far as he knew, Patricia's cause of death had been a massive stroke, and she'd never tell him otherwise. In addition to protecting their magical secret, Stevie wanted to spare him the truth of his wife's death. It would only add anger to his grief, just as it had for her. A combination she wouldn't wish on anyone. Certainly not her father.

Stevie tossed a load of laundry in the washing machine and then went to work tidying up the already immaculate cottage.

Charlie sat on the floor, playing with his small cars and stuffed animals. In quiet concentration, he arranged them all in a straight line, from tallest to shortest. Stevie glanced at her father and realized that he too had noticed what Charlie had done. Neither one said anything about it. She knew her son was attempting to seek order in a world that often did not make sense. If lining up his toys gave him peace, so be it.

When the chime on the washing machine dinged, Stevie shifted the laundry over to the dryer.

In spite of her father's protests, she decided to prepare dinner anyway, with the hope of using up some of the food provided by thoughtful neighbors and friends. She swung the refrigerator door open and perused its contents. Jim had been right; the shelves and bins were loaded with casseroles and hams.

Nothing says "sorry for your loss" quite like a hunk of spiral sliced sympathy.

Stevie reheated green beans, mashed potatoes, and a few slices of ham for the three of them. After she set the table, she called for Jim and Charlie to join her in the kitchen.

She didn't have much of an appetite, so she busied herself by pushing her food around her plate. Right away, she realized her father was engrossed in the same tactic.

"Dad, you have to eat something." She pointed her fork at his food.

Jim took in the sight of Stevie's plate and narrowed his eyes, as if beginning a shrewd negotiation. "You first."

"Fine." Stevie shoveled a forkful of mashed potatoes into her mouth. "Your turn," she said with her mouth still full.

He complied and ate a couple of green beans. While he chewed, he nodded toward Stevie.

Back and forth, they continued in this fashion for another couple of rounds. Neither had consumed enough to fill their bellies, but it was enough to reduce Stevie's worries for his well-being. At least for the evening. After dinner, Jim and Charlie returned to the den to watch cartoons while she cleaned the kitchen.

The buzzer on the dryer sounded. Stevie finished wiping down the kitchen counter and then went to the laundry room to retrieve the clothes. She carried the pile in a plastic hamper to her parents' bedroom and placed it on the bed.

Stevie plucked one of Patricia's trademark ankle-length dresses from the warm heap of clothes. With a whimsical swirl embroidered along its hem, the cotton frock had been one of her mother's favorites. Stevie held it close and allowed some of her tears to fall.

She took in a deep breath to compose herself and then made her way across the room to hang up the dress. The old closet door sailed open with a creak as she approached.

A sudden rush of electric energy pulsed through her, commanding her attention. She froze and scanned the contents of the closet in search of the magic she sensed. Studying her mother's collection of dresses and sandals, she noticed nothing unusual about them. Even the hatboxes and bins that lined the top shelf were unremarkable.

She dipped her head down, eyeing the floor, and her energy surged once again. This time with an effervescence she'd never experienced before. Her heart thudded with anticipation. Tucked beneath the hems of several sundresses sat a plastic bin. Its subtle glow called to her. *Magic.* She hastily draped her mother's dress on a hanger and then knelt down in front of the container to investigate.

Right away, she lifted the lid and peeked inside to find her mother's collection of Fleetwood Mac music. Some of the albums were duplicates that Patricia had purchased over the years as technological advances created new ways of enjoying music. Vinyl records, cassette tapes, and compact discs stood in neat stacks at the bottom of the container.

The magical pull continued, urging her to see beyond the obvious contents of the bin. There was something more. She just had to search for it.

She reached in and began to thumb through the stack of albums until her fingers brushed against the corner of an envelope tucked in between two old records. She gave it a tug and pulled it out.

The bubbling sensation came to a sudden halt, abandoning her without warning, and she knew she'd found the object she was supposed to discover. Stevie swept her hand across the front of the envelope, which bore her name in her mother's handwriting. She clutched it to her chest and blinked back hot tears.

Her father's heavy footsteps sounded on the wooden floorboards of the hallway as he approached the bedroom. Instinctively, Stevie knew she shouldn't open the envelope in front of him. She tucked it in the back pocket of her jeans and hustled back to the mundane work of folding laundry just as he plodded into the room.

Whatever the envelope contained, Patricia had made sure Stevie would find it. She couldn't wait to get home and open it.

Chapter four

Vanessa

The sun had set on Beaufort. From a seat on the deck of her yacht, Vanessa watched as the small town settled in for the night. The stores along Front Street darkened one by one as business owners turned off their lights and closed their shops for the day.

A few Friday night revelers roamed the quiet street in search of a bar to celebrate the end of a grueling workweek. With the exception of distant chatter or an occasional laugh, silence prevailed. Even Susan, who lounged in a nearby chaise, nursed her martini without comment. For once.

The edge of Vanessa's black hood flapped in the cool, salty breeze, and she winced as it brushed against her burned cheek. Still tender and raw, her face had not yet healed as much as the less severe wounds that stretched along her left arm. Another gust kicked up and whisked the cover away from her forehead, almost exposing the choppy patches of hair and gnarled scars on her scalp. With a start, she reached up, grasped the hood, and tugged it back into place.

Her mother snorted. "I saw that."

When she was feeling generous, Susan blamed Vanessa's burns on the unbridled tyranny of the coven. But she hadn't had a spell of generosity in at least three drinks. Vanessa closed her eyes for a long moment, bracing herself for the alcohol-infused verbal beating that was sure to come next.

Susan swung her glass in a sloppy, wide-sweeping gesture. "Hideous and weak…that's what you are now." She took care to enunciate her descriptors amid the mishmash of slurred words, as if it were a statement Vanessa hadn't already heard countless times that day.

As before, Vanessa accepted the hurled insults in silence. Attempting to defend herself would only serve to rile her mother more.

After a sip of her martini, Susan leaned back against the padded headrest of the chaise lounge. She cupped her hand around the amethyst amulet and stared at the night sky. "Did I tell you what this thing does?" She did not pause in expectation of an answer. "It lets me see what the other queens saw. I have their memories now, and I can see all of their magic and rituals. I know their *secrets*."

Her mother's words tumbled forth, soft around the edges. Vanessa didn't enjoy seeing Susan in this state, but she held out hope that it would work in her favor. Perhaps her mother would get drunk enough to agree to restore Vanessa's powers or, at least, disguise her grotesque burns. At this point, she'd be grateful for a remedy to either problem.

She bit her lip and considered what she would do if her mother passed out from her copious alcohol consumption. The idea played out as a fantasy in her mind. Nothing more than a dream really. She shook away the thought almost as soon as it entered her mind. She could never attempt to steal the amulet. *Too risky.* If Susan caught her, there would be no end to the punishment that woman would dole out. Vanessa couldn't imagine a situation more miserable than the one she currently endured, but she had no doubt her mother could find a way to make it worse.

Susan sat upright again and lifted a pair of binoculars from the table next to her. Without a word, she raised them to her eyes and peered toward the western end of Front Street, in the direction of Stevie's house.

Vanessa followed her mother's line of sight and saw only buildings and trees obscuring the view. She tilted her head, confused at first. But then she realized right away that Susan must have had a clear view of the house. With the help of the amulet, she could accomplish almost anything. *Seeing through trees and buildings is probably child's play to her now.*

Vanessa's lips pursed as a twinge of envy struck. She'd give anything to have that kind of power herself.

"It appears Stevie has company. I see someone walking up to her door." Susan leaned forward, as if to get a better look. "You have got to be kidding me!"

Vanessa jumped from her chair and rushed to her mother's side. "What's going on?"

"Stevie has a basket on her porch, and that woman just left a gift in it for her." Susan spoke with the sort of indignation reminiscent of a tattling child.

Vanessa furrowed her brow. "What's the problem? She was probably just leaving something to express her condolences over Patricia's death. No big deal."

Susan smacked the binoculars back down on the table and then took another swallow of her martini. "It's a custom from ancient times. When a queen dies, the successor leaves a basket for her people to leave offerings honoring her as the new queen. They usually leave small items like handmade candles or soaps, often with a spell attached for the new queen's protection or health. It's how they show their loyalty." She polished off the rest of her drink with an unceremonious gulp. "By accepting these gifts, Stevie has declared herself *queen*."

Vanessa sighed and strolled back to her seat. Stevie was even bolder than she'd thought.

"They should be leaving those gifts for me!" Susan bared her teeth and jerked her thumb toward her chest. "I'm their new queen!"

Vanessa lowered her head. Her mother was as angry as ever. There was no chance she'd fall into a blissful, benevolent state of inebriation now.

Susan heaved herself up from the chaise and grabbed the railing to steady herself. "You know what this means, don't you?" She didn't wait for an answer. "Obviously, I can't allow this to continue. I'm going to have to kill her much sooner than I had originally planned. I won't be able to play with her first." She scowled. "Kind of takes all the fun out of it."

Sensing an opportunity, Vanessa raised her chin. "Mother, if you restore my powers, I could help you settle this."

Susan cackled. "Oh, do you really think I need help? Do you think I need *your* help?" She cupped the amethyst again. "This is all the help I need. I know everything about the coven now, including their *special* talents."

Vanessa arched what remained of her eyebrow. She had no specific knowledge of special talents among the coven members—she only suspected they had some. Ignoring the venom in her mother's words, she listened, waiting for any tidbits of information that might prove useful.

Susan attempted to step forward but only managed an inelegant stumble. "I can even see how they bound your powers. They performed an old ritual that required a group effort." Her head bobbed as she spoke. "They wrapped a black string around a photo of you, and each one took part in the spell that left you this way. *All* of them participated—remember that." Susan smirked and jabbed her finger in Vanessa's general direction. "Then they packed it away in a safe."

Vanessa's breath caught in her throat. "Do you know where they keep the safe?"

"I can only see what Patricia saw. She didn't hide the safe herself. She gave it to Dylan and told him to sink it."

"Sink it? So it's in the water then." Vanessa's eyes grew wide as she gazed out over Taylor's Creek, black as oil beneath the dark sky. "It's close."

"Probably. When I feel that you have *earned* it, I'll cast a seeking spell so we can pinpoint the location. Once we find it, restoring your power is a very simple matter." She waggled her empty martini glass in Vanessa's direction. "Now be a good girl and fix me another drink."

A knot twisted in Vanessa's stomach, but she complied. She had to keep her mother happy if she wanted her powers restored. *I have to earn it.*

When she returned to the deck to deliver the drink, her mother accepted the glass without uttering a "thank you." Hiding her disgust beneath a half-smile, Vanessa retreated to the yacht's cabin and stepped into her room. Susan couldn't demean her in the solace of her private quarters.

She spotted a plain ivory pillar candle on her nightstand. It had sat, unnoticed and unused since an interior decorator placed it there sometime before she'd purchased the yacht. It's white wick stood tall at the center of the candle.

What if…

Vanessa recalled her earliest days as a young witch and the simple spells she'd practiced back then. If any magic remained within her, she needed to know. *It can't hurt to try.* She focused on the wick and envisioned an orange flame igniting.

Nothing happened.

She tried again. This time, she squeezed her eyes shut, forcing all of her concentration on the candle. Employing every bit of mental imagery she possessed, Vanessa heard the whoosh of the tiny flame and caught a whiff of its narrow plume of smoke. She held the image in her mind for a long moment, reveling in its power.

She opened her eyes, expecting to witness success. But the wick remained unlit, as pristine as it had been when she'd first noticed it. Her shoulders slumped. She couldn't even manage a simple parlor trick.

The spark of hope extinguished just as fast as her mental image of the burning candle. She'd been wrong to assume it wouldn't hurt to try. It *had* hurt—just in a way she hadn't expected. Vanessa crawled into her bed, resigned to the loathsome fact that serving her mother was the only way she'd ever get her powers back.

Chapter five

Stevie

Late Friday night, Stevie entered her bedroom. After waiting all evening for a moment alone to read her mother's letter, the opportunity had finally come. She pulled the folded envelope from the back pocket of her jeans and sat down on the edge of her bed. She paused before opening it, listening to the sounds of her household. Without knowing the contents of the letter, she didn't want to risk an unexpected interruption.

Since her powers developed, Stevie had noticed an undeniable enhancement in her sensory perception. Sights, sounds, and smells now presented with a clarity she had never known before. She held her breath, listening for any hints of possible interruption.

A steady procession of creaks came from the downstairs hallway as Dylan paced along its wooden floorboards. He'd insisted on staying with her and Charlie since the night Patricia died. She'd offered him one of the guest rooms, but he rarely used it. Instead, he spent his nights doing what he could to protect them from their merciless foe. She heard him turn the knob on the front door to check the lock before resuming his patrol of the old house.

She listened to Charlie's deep, even inhalations as he slept in his room across the hall. She still didn't know if he understood the permanence of his grandmother's death. Any small child would have difficulty grasping the concept, but his limited communication skills made it harder for her to assess his comprehension of the situation. Stevie sighed. One way or another, she'd have to find a way to help him process the loss. But she didn't even know how to get through it herself.

She stared down at the envelope, resisting the urge to tear it open. Whatever its contents, this would be the last communication she would ever receive from her mother. She didn't want to damage it. With only a small amount of focused magical intent, she dissolved the adhesive seal and gently raised the flap.

Stevie removed the single sheet of paper and placed the envelope next to her on the bed. Her hands trembled as she unfolded the stationery, taking in the sight of her mother's final message. The date in the top right corner of the letter caught her eye.

Her mother had written the note two weeks earlier, at the end of September, before Susan had orchestrated the theft of the amulet. She continued reading.

> *My dear Stevie,*
>   *I didn't inherit Lucia's well-honed gift of foresight. Instead, I only have a nagging intuition and the life experience to know to listen to it. I write this now because I sense I am nearing the end of my time here. I don't know*

exactly how or when I'll meet my demise, but I suspect the day is fast approaching.

By the time you read this, I will have passed on to the other side. Surely, the amulet has already revealed to you the mysteries of our afterlife. I hope you find comfort in the knowledge that I'm with our ancestors, and one day, we will be together again.

The amulet has probably also shown you how to communicate with me. You must resist that urge! Our people are no longer strong enough to manage that type of magic.

If you attempt to open the veil, you risk allowing dark souls passage back into the world. It's simply too dangerous. Keep the veil closed…always.

If my intuition holds true, we won't have had much time to practice your skills, and I'm sure you still have a lot of questions. Regardless, you are ready to lead our people. Your loyal coven will assist you with anything you need, and the amulet will provide you with knowledge and power. Remember—you were born to be a queen.

I love you with all of my heart,

Mom

P.S. Yes, you have to preside over the Historical Society too.

Stevie couldn't help but smile as she read the last line of the letter. Her mother had known her so well.

The sound of Dylan's footsteps in the upstairs hallway caught her attention. She looked up just as he reached her doorway.

He tilted his head, brow knitted with concern. "Are you okay?"

"I'm fine." She folded the letter and returned it to the envelope.

Dylan stepped closer to her. "You've been crying."

Stevie touched her cheek to find it wet with tears. "I guess I have. I didn't realize…"

He settled next to her on the bed and wrapped his arm around her. "I'm here, you know. You don't have to go through this alone."

"I know," she said as she dried her tears with a swipe of her hand. "I'm okay. Really, I am." She rested her head against his shoulder.

"What's this?" He pointed to the envelope.

"A pep talk from my mom. She wrote it weeks ago." Stevie inhaled a deep breath. "She knew she was going to die."

Dylan remained silent for a long moment before he spoke. "Are you saying she knew Susan was coming back?"

"No." Stevie shook her head. "Nothing that specific. In fact, it's clear she expected I would inherit the amulet. She wrote about some sort of veil. I have no idea what that means."

Stevie rose from the bed and walked over to her dresser. She opened her small jewelry box, which held more keepsakes than baubles, and tucked the envelope inside. Someday, maybe time would ease her pain, and she would read the letter again. Maybe it would become a cherished reminder of her mother, one that brought only smiles instead of tears. For now, however, she didn't want to think about her loss. She didn't want to worry about her responsibilities as the new queen. And, she certainly didn't want to consider her new position as president of the Beaufort Historic Society.

Dylan stood up. "I'll let you get to sleep. The queen needs her rest." He grinned as he started to leave her room.

"Dylan, wait." Stevie stepped toward him.

He turned as she approached. Standing before him, she rose up on her toes. She placed her hands on his cheeks and then pulled his face down toward hers to give him a fierce kiss.

He pulled back. "Stevie, are you sure? It hasn't been that long since..."

She didn't let him finish his sentence. Instead, she kissed him again.

It had taken some time for her to feel comfortable with him again after Susan's attack, but she was ready to put that behind her. She had the real Dylan in her bedroom now. Of that, she had no doubt. He would never hurt her.

"I'm sure."

Chapter Six

Stevie

Stevie stood in the center of her store sorting through a new order of postcards that featured some of her latest black and white prints. Without a single customer so far, it had been a slow Saturday morning. During the summer months, tourists flocked to Coastal Visions to admire Lexi's original watercolor paintings and Stevie's photography. But as the temperature outside dropped, visitors to the area decreased. She didn't mind the seasonal ebb and flow of the business. It was all part of living on the coast.

Besides, the lull in traffic gave her the opportunity to busy herself with mundane organizational chores, a task she preferred much more than sitting in her house under the guard of revolving coven members. When her store manager called and asked for the morning off, Stevie had jumped at the opportunity to fill in for her. Working, even if only for a few hours, came as a welcome distraction from her grief and worry.

Charlie had settled in a chair next to the window display, content to play games on his tablet while Stevie restocked the circular rack of postcards and stationery.

Spending time in Coastal Visions reminded her of a different time in her life. Not so long ago, she'd been a mom and a business owner. She sighed. *Simpler times.* Now, in addition to those roles, she was a witch, a queen, and—to her unceasing dismay—the new president of The Beaufort Historic Society.

Stevie glanced at Lexi's latest addition to the store, a painting of a pod of dolphins jumping and swimming in Taylor's Creek. She recalled a sunny summer day when she and Charlie had visited Carrot Island. She'd watched dolphins playing in the water while Charlie sifted sand through his hands. Thinking back on it now, she realized just how comfortable she had been in her blissful oblivion.

The bell on the front door chimed as it swung open, and Lexi bustled in with a smile. In spite of her hurried demeanor, the choreography of her bleached-blond pixie cut remained flawless. She wore a slim fitting, knee-length dress with cap sleeves along with high heels that made Stevie cringe at the mere thought of trying to walk in them.

"Hey, Charlie," Lexi called over her shoulder as she entered the shop. She stopped suddenly before the door swung itself closed behind her. "Oh, shoot!" She slapped her hand against her thigh.

"What's wrong?" Stevie asked.

"I forgot to bring the sea salt with me. I still need to put it around the outside of the shop."

Stevie dismissed Lexi's concern with a wave of her hand. "I'm sure we'll be fine without it. But then again, it might come in handy if we're suddenly invaded by murderous slugs." She flashed a sardonic grin.

"Make fun of it if you want to." Lexi wagged her finger. "But you have to admit that you've had no unwelcome visitors at your house since I put the salt down."

"True." Stevie had no interest in arguing with Lexi. Her best friend's heart, as usual, was in the right place, so she decided to change the subject. "I wasn't expecting you to come in today. Did you know I was here?"

Lexi's high heels clicked on the floorboards as she made her way to Stevie. "Dylan said you were here." She placed her hand on her hip and narrowed her eyes. "He also said you wouldn't let him come with you."

"I don't suppose he mentioned that I said I'd be fine on my own." It hadn't been easy to convince Dylan to stay behind that morning, but she'd wanted him to have a break from guarding her. More than that, she'd wanted a break from being guarded. "I don't need you guys babysitting me all the time."

Lexi relaxed her arm and smiled. "I just came by to sort some of the new stock in the backroom. I'm definitely not here to *babysit*." She twirled around and proceeded to walk to the rear of the store.

"Liar."

Lexi giggled in response as she disappeared into the backroom.

Stevie shook her head and spun the rack that she'd been organizing for a final check. Satisfied with her work, she stepped behind the checkout counter and grabbed a bottle of water from the small refrigerator beneath the cash register. "Are you thirsty, Charlie?"

He glanced up from his tablet but paused as though deep in thought. Stevie tilted her head, confused by his hesitation. She'd asked this question countless times. He must have understood her.

He shook his head and returned his attention to his game once more. Stevie almost wished she'd allowed Dylan to join them today. With his ability to read thoughts, he could have explained the delay in Charlie's response. Stevie shrugged it off. There would always be times when she wished she knew what Charlie was thinking. She took a sip of her water and then placed the bottle on the counter.

The natural light coming through the picture window at the front of the store suddenly dimmed, so she walked toward it to catch a glimpse of the sky. Rain poured down on Carrot Island, and black storm clouds soared overhead toward Front Street. The leading edge of the squall had already begun to race across Taylor's Creek. It would arrive in Beaufort within seconds.

A blustery gust of wind blew, creating a white-capped chop on the water. Boats secured at the dock across the street began to rock as the waves came in. Stevie's gaze fell on Vanessa's yacht, where she saw someone standing on its deck.

Susan stared back at Stevie, with a glare that fixed the new queen in place like a butterfly pinned to a board.

A chill, born at the nape of Stevie's neck, raced down her spine. She regretted scoffing at Lexi's salt line moments earlier. She pulled her focus away from Susan to check on Charlie. He looked up from his tablet, his brow furrowed with concern. Though he hadn't seen the danger in their midst, she suspected he'd sensed the change in her emotional state.

"I am okay, Charlie," she lied. "Play your game."

Stevie's initial fear gave way to a rush of anger as she turned toward the yacht once more. Fueled by her devotion to her people, she took in the full hate of Susan's sneer and mirrored it with her own furious glare.

Stevie raised her chin in defiance and considered destroying the yacht with both of its inhabitants on board. She could think of nothing more satisfying than eliminating the dark witch in a blazing fire. Even if she were unable to recover the amulet, having Susan out of her life would be worth the sacrifice. She and Charlie could live without fear. Her beloved coven would be free to enjoy the rest of their days in safety. Beaufort would once again be the coastal oasis she had always loved.

Susan abruptly abandoned the deck of the yacht and disappeared into its cabin as the advancing downpour neared the dock. Her movement jolted Stevie out of her fantasy and forced her back into an unwelcome reality. Her daydream shattered under the weight of logic and undeniable truths. Yes, she had the power to set the yacht ablaze, but she couldn't guarantee the safety of the innocents nearby. She had no way to control who would get hurt if she took such an action. *I can't take that risk.*

The sheet of driving rain pushed across the boats at the dock and then across the street, until it arrived at Stevie's shop. Heavy droplets crashed onto the roof of the store, thunderous and incessant. Charlie cast a wary glance through the window.

"Don't worry. We'll go home soon." She patted his back.

Lexi emerged from the backroom carrying a box. "Whoa! That's some storm, huh?" She set the box on top of a display table near the center of the store. "The lighthouse books came in." She began to stack the books on the table.

Tempted to tell Lexi about her encounter with Susan, Stevie bit down on her lip and shook away the idea. *Nothing good would come from it.* If anything, telling Lexi would only serve to confirm the belief that she must have another witch protecting her at all times.

Stevie walked over to Lexi and pulled one of the oversized, hardcover books from the box. She ran her hand across its glossy cover and then turned it over. The back cover promised readers would learn all about the lighthouses that dotted the North Carolina coastline.

"I'll put one in the front display." Stevie crossed the store and stood the book upright on the window shelf. Before she had a chance to turn away, Charlie abandoned his tablet and grabbed the book. He opened it on his lap, settling on a page of colorful photographs. Stevie chuckled and tousled her little boy's curls. "Okay then. I'll just get another one for the display."

Unexpected movement on the other side of the window caught Stevie's eye. She turned her head to get a better look and found Sam standing beneath the store's overhang, sheltering himself from the sudden storm. Fat raindrops spattered his jacket and dripped from his shaggy blond hair. When he waved at Stevie, she swung the door open for him.

Sam stood on the walkway in front of the store and brushed the excess water from his clothes. "I was heading to Clawson's to grab lunch with a friend and got caught in the rain."

With a friend? It seemed odd to Stevie that he didn't mention *who* he was planning to meet since they basically had all the same friends.

He shook his head, hurling droplets in every direction. "That storm came out of nowhere. Good thing I'm running early." He unzipped his jacket to reveal an unwrinkled button down shirt.

Barring attendance at weddings and funerals, Sam lived in t-shirts. The starched collar was a dead giveaway. *He has a date.* In spite of her curiosity—and happiness for him—she decided not to ask him about it, opting instead to continue their discussion of the weather. "It came in across the water, moving really fast. Probably won't last too long." *He can tell me when he's ready.*

"That's good." Sam dried the bottoms of his shoes on the outdoor mat. "I booked a few customers for this afternoon since Charlie isn't staying with me. I hope it clears up soon so I can keep those appointments."

She'd spoken with Sam on the phone just the day before to ask if they could skip Charlie's usual weekend visit. Stevie didn't tell him that she couldn't let Charlie out of her sight while Susan roamed free in Beaufort. As far as he knew, the reason for her request had been Patricia's death, and he'd accepted that excuse without making a fuss. Despite all of their missteps in the early months of their divorce, they'd finally settled into a comfortable routine of co-parenting. For that, Stevie was grateful.

"Come on in and dry off." Stevie pulled the door open wider and gestured for him to enter.

Sam stomped his boat shoes against the mat a final time before he entered the shop and eased toward Charlie. "Reading up on lighthouses, huh?" He tilted his head to view the page. "You know that one, don't you?" He pointed to the image of the lighthouse with the black and white diamond pattern. "That's our lighthouse at Cape Lookout."

Charlie nodded.

"We should go out there sometime soon, Charlie. Now that you're a big boy, we can climb the steps all the way to the top of the lighthouse, if you want." Sam flashed a crooked grin at Stevie. "What do you think?"

"Sure."

Stevie did her best to mask her worry with a forced smile. She couldn't let that trip happen anytime soon. It would have to wait until she'd eliminated Susan as a threat. Assuming she could.

Chapter seven

Stevie

That evening, Stevie sat at her kitchen table watching Alice Gillikin sort through the enormous pile of gifts that had accumulated in the basket. Lines, from a long lifetime of smiles, curved along Alice's chubby cheeks, and her friendly brown eyes lit up as she retrieved each new gift from the pile. She hummed while she worked, but Stevie didn't recognize the tune.

Sorting the gifts by type, she positioned the homemade candles along the far edge of the table and then stacked the fragrant soaps in the center. She separated the sachets of herbs from the dry tea blends. Miscellaneous items that didn't quite fit into one category or another formed a grouping of their own.

"Oh," Alice cooed as she plucked a gemstone from the pile and placed it on the table. Translucent and iridescent at once, it had a rounded top and a flat bottom. Stevie had never seen anything quite like it before.

"Go ahead, dear. Pick it up." Alice gestured toward it. "That one is my favorite." She resumed her search through the basket, selecting various stones from inside. She set each one in front of Stevie.

Stevie grasped the unusual rock and placed it on her palm. Cool to the touch, it emitted a strange energy. She stroked its round edges, enjoying the tingle it sent through her fingers. "What's it called?"

"That's a moonstone." Alice straightened the array of gems she had placed on the table. "It's connected to our feminine energy as well as the moon. That piece would make a lovely ring, don't you think?"

Stevie nodded as she continued to stroke it, savoring the unexpected surge of peaceful energy it bestowed upon her. She took in the sight of the other baubles Alice had assembled. Some, like the amethyst and turquoise, she recognized. Others were somewhat familiar to her, but she didn't know their names or purposes.

I still have so much to learn.

With reluctance, she returned the moonstone to the table and pointed to a jagged rock with a metallic sheen. "What's that one?"

"Hematite." Alice lifted the silvery gray mineral. "I like to use this one for healing and protective magic." She returned it to the table. "All of them have multiple uses. I find that what works well for one witch may not work as well for another. So, there's a bit of trial and error. It's somewhat complicated, but I can help you sort it all out."

Dylan came to stand in the kitchen doorway. Leaning against the doorframe with his arms crossed, he watched the impromptu class with a grin.

"I may not know much about this stuff, but I know that one isn't a jewel." Stevie pointed to small piece of green sea glass that Alice had placed among the stones.

"You are quite right, dear," Alice replied. "But it's magical nonetheless. Pick it up."

Dubious, Stevie narrowed her eyes. In her lifetime on the coast, she had collected countless similar pieces. Though she'd always admired their simple beauty, she had never sensed anything particularly special about them. But then again, she hadn't touched a piece of sea glass since her powers manifested.

Stevie glanced at Alice, who watched with a gleam in her eye, and then wrapped her fingers around the thin piece of green glass. In an instant, the energy it contained bolted through her entire body, as if propelled by the full power of the ocean. Stevie sucked in a sharp breath before a sudden burst of peace washed over her. Calm and still, she could almost hear the wisdom of the ages whispered on the ocean breeze.

Everything she experienced whenever she was on the water now rested in the palm of her hand. Vitality. Tranquility. Wisdom.

"Our people are strongest when we're near water. So, it stands to reason that any product of the ocean would have an impact on us. However, sea glass is extra special."

Stevie arched her eyebrow. "How so?"

"Think about how glass is made. It begins as sand and minerals, which are of the earth. Then they're subjected to fire in order to be melted and shaped. Eventually, the glass finds its way to the ocean, where it's smoothed in waves powered by wind."

Stevie turned the thin sea glass around in her hand, admiring the texture of its matte finish. "All four elements—earth, air, fire, and water."

"Exactly!" Alice beamed.

Dylan cleared his throat. "You're a natural born teacher, Alice."

The older witch turned her head toward him. "It's funny you should say that." She tucked one of her white curls behind her ear as a blush crept into her cheeks. "I've been a coven member during the reign of three different queens now. In that time, I have amassed a good deal of knowledge, and I do enjoy sharing what I've learned." She paused and dipped her chin. "It's always been a dream of mine to start a school for young witches."

"Sounds like a worthy cause to me." His amiable grin revealed dimples on either side of his full lips. "I'd be happy to fund that venture."

"Really? Oh my." Alice raised her hand to her chest. "I—I couldn't accept…well, yes, I suppose I could. How generous!" She threw her plump arms around his neck. "You've always been such a sweet boy!" She planted a loud kiss on his cheek. "I accept your offer."

"Good." Dylan peeled himself away from Alice's embrace. "We'll get to work on it as soon as we've handled this *situation* with Susan."

Stevie thought he was too optimistic regarding their "situation with Susan," but she bit her tongue. She enjoyed seeing her coven members happy, even if their joy stemmed from naiveté.

Alice buzzed with excitement as she returned to her lesson and pointed to another gemstone. Bright blue in color with a band of tan and gold flecks along its bottom edge, it reminded Stevie of the view of the ocean from the beach.

"This one is lapis lazuli," the elder witch explained. "It's good for improving your mood, among other things."

Alice emptied the basket while Stevie surveyed the variety of gifts now laid out on her kitchen table. The witches of Beaufort had been generous in welcoming her as their new queen. Their offerings had all been thoughtful, but the gifts designed to ease her grief warmed her heart the most.

"This one is pretty." She reached for an oblong pink crystal.

Alice turned to Dylan. "Sweetie, would you put this basket back out on the porch for me?"

"Of course."

As soon as Dylan disappeared from the doorway, Alice leaned in close to Stevie and pointed to the pink crystal. "That's rose quartz. It helps with fertility." She spoke in a conspiratorial whisper, adding a wink for good measure.

Stevie pursed her lips and returned the crystal to the table. "Oh—I don't need that one. I'm not having any more children."

Alice's smile disappeared, and her eyes grew wide. "Don't be silly. Of course you will. There has *always* been a girl child to succeed the queen."

Stevie opened her mouth to reply, but Dylan returned to the kitchen before she had a chance to speak. He carried a single ivory pillar candle. "This was on the porch."

"Let me see what you have there." Alice held out her hand to receive the candle from Dylan. She scanned its plain, waxy surface. "I don't see any herbs in there." She held it up to her nose and sniffed. "No essential oils either." She wrapped both hands around the pillar and blinked. "Strange." She tilted her head. "This is store bought. I sense no magic in it all."

Alice passed the candle to Stevie and then turned to Dylan. "Was there a card with it?"

Dylan shook his head. "There was nothing else out there."

Stevie turned the pillar over. Someone had carved a "V" into the smooth skin of its base. Her blood ran cold. There was only one witch in town who could have left this gift for her. She dropped the candle as though it had burned her.

Dylan was at her side in an instant. "Stevie? Are you okay?"

She stayed quiet for a long moment, staring at the gift as she sought the best way to make her confession. "I have something to tell you."

She drew in a deep breath and began talking. She told them about Vanessa's shocking return as well as her gruesome scars. And she shared how Vanessa had warned her to take Charlie and leave town. "I don't know if her warning was truly intended to protect Charlie or if it was all part of some scheme to intimidate me. Whatever the case, I don't trust her."

Dylan sunk into a chair on the opposite side of the table. He wouldn't meet her gaze. Stevie saw his jaw clench.

"I'm sorry. I should have told you." She traced the edge of one of the table's tiles with her finger. "When I saw her…what I did to her…I just didn't know what to do." She looked at Dylan. "You were gone and then my mom…"

"What's done is done." Alice clasped her hands together. "It's strange though; this candle suggests that her powers are still bound. Why hasn't Susan restored them yet? If she'd let Vanessa wear the amulet for a moment, our binding ritual would have been undone. Remember how your mother left it for you to find? She did that to give you a little nudge. It worked perfectly."

Stevie shook her head. "I don't know if we'll ever fully understand Susan, but I'd bet she doesn't trust her own daughter with the amulet."

"That pendant contains the memories and spells of all of the queens. Susan is now privy to the binding spell we used. If she is unwilling to share it, she could easily locate the sunken safe that contains Vanessa's bound powers. Vanessa would only need to unwind the black string we wrapped around her photograph to get her powers back."

"What?" Stevie hunched forward, slack-jawed. "I distinctly remember chanting 'our magic today cannot be undone.' How is it possible that her powers are so easily restored?"

"Those old rhyming spells are full of quirks. Honestly, if Susan hadn't stolen the amulet, it would be extremely difficult, if not impossible, for Vanessa to regain her powers. One of us would have had to bring up the safe *and* open it for her," Alice explained. "That would have never happened."

Stevie gulped. Without a word, she reached forward and picked up the ivory candle.

Alice placed her hand on Stevie's shoulder. "Now honey, don't think you can trust her just because she left a gift for you. It might be a trick."

"I know. I'm just thinking." Stevie rolled the pillar back and forth between her hands.

Dylan's back stiffened as he watched Stevie. "You're not seriously considering giving Vanessa her powers back, are you?"

"Of course not!" The very thought left a bitter taste in Stevie's mouth. She plopped the candle down on the table. "What if I opened the safe and unwound the black string? Would *I* take on her powers?"

Alice pressed her lips together in a thin line. "I don't think that has ever been attempted before, but, yes, I suppose you would."

Stevie continued contemplating her idea. "I'm so weak compared to Susan. If I had more magic, maybe we would stand a chance of beating her."

"We don't know what those dark powers would do to you, Stevie." Dylan leaned in, locking eyes with her. "It's not worth the risk."

"Vanessa's magic wasn't dark," Alice said to Dylan. "Her gifts were as pure as ours. It's how she chose to use her power that made her evil."

He shook his head. "We don't know that for sure."

Alice sighed. "Well, in any case, I have to advise against this, Stevie. You may not be strong enough to manage that much magic yet. The results could be catastrophic."

"You have the full support of the coven. You don't need Vanessa's powers. And, from the look of it," Dylan gestured at the bounty of gifts on the table, "if the other witches in town knew what was going on, they would support you as well."

Stevie picked up the piece of sea glass and rubbed her thumb across its surface. She considered the effect it had on her. As powerful as it was, she knew it was nothing compared to the strength of the amulet.

"It's not enough." Stevie slipped the sea glass into the pocket of her jeans.

Alice patted her shoulder. "We'll figure something out, dear."

Stevie's thoughts shifted to the safe she and Dylan had dropped in Taylor's Creek. For the first time since her mother's death, she felt a glimmer of hope. In spite of Alice's warning, she wasn't ready to let go of the idea. Absorbing Vanessa's powers, dark or not, may very well be the only way she could protect her people.

It's worth the risk.

Chapter eight

Vanessa

Determined to enjoy herself while Susan was away, Vanessa stood in front of the tall, built-in bookcase in the main cabin of her yacht. She scanned the titles in search of something to read, only to reject one novel after another. She'd already read most of them, and the few that remained didn't command her interest. She sighed. There was a bookstore just across the street from the dock. If she weren't so ashamed of her scars, she could walk over and select something new. She shook off the thought and plucked the television remote from the coffee table.

While she sifted through a hundred channels of nothing-to-watch, the cabin door slammed behind her. *She's back.* Vanessa cringed. Her quiet evening alone was over, far earlier than she'd hoped. Given the forcefulness of Susan's entry, she knew she was about to get an earful about her mother's chats with the some of the town's witches. Whether she wanted it or not.

Susan began to pace the length of the yacht's living area, punctuating her steps with heavy stomps as she went. Her narrow face contorted into a scowl that left new wrinkles etched around her mouth.

Vanessa peered at Susan with a sidelong glance, bracing herself for the inevitable tirade. She didn't have to wait long.

"They don't believe me!" Susan shouted, throwing her hands up in the air in disbelief. "I told *two* witches that I am their new queen." She shook her head as she continued to pace. "They all but laughed at me!"

She halted her furious stomping and whipped around to address Vanessa. "I saw them, a man and a woman, walking on the boardwalk. I could tell by their auras that they weren't as strong as we are." She stopped, realizing her error. "I mean, they weren't as strong as *I* am. But they were definitely witches. I showed them the amulet and told them what it meant."

"What did they say?"

"Nothing!" Susan's lips pursed. "They gawked at me like I had two heads and then just walked away. Can you believe that? They walked away from *me*!"

"Did you...um..." Vanessa struggled to find acceptable phrasing for her question. "Are they still alive?"

Susan rolled her eyes. "Yes, of course they're still alive. It won't help my cause to start killing off the witches in town. Though I do foresee an unfortunate accident coming their way after I settle the business of being properly acknowledged as the queen."

Vanessa thought for a moment before speaking, wondering if she could diffuse Susan's growing rage with logic. "You can't really blame them, Mother. The women of Stevie's family have always led the witches. You'd be hard pressed to convince anyone otherwise."

"But I have the amulet!" Susan's knuckles blanched as she tightened her grip on the pendant.

Vanessa continued to keep her tone calm, trying to be the voice of reason in a most unreasonable situation. "I told you, most of the witches don't even know about that necklace. It hardly serves as proof from their standpoint."

"I'll show them!" Susan released her hold on the amethyst and let her hand fall to her side. "I'll show them all."

Vanessa nodded. "I'm sure you will."

Susan's eyes flicked back and forth. Vanessa could only imagine the violent scenarios that were playing out in the theater of her mother's mind.

"It won't be enough just to kill Stevie and the boy. I'll have to demonstrate my power too." Susan turned to the window and stared through it with a far off look in her eyes. "They need to know what I can do."

Vanessa arched her eyebrow. "What do you have in mind?"

"I'm still working out some of the details, but I'll tell you all about it soon." Her scowl slowly gave way to a chill-inducing sneer. "In the meantime, we'll keep spreading the word that I'm the new queen."

"We?" Vanessa raised her hand to her scarred cheek. "I'm not ready to be out in public. Not like this anyway." She hoped her mother would recognize the obvious solution to this problem.

"Those scars are exactly why I need you to come with me. The witches need to know what Stevie did to you. Once they know how evil she is, they'll be more likely to accept me as their queen." Susan tilted her head as she studied Vanessa's scars. "Actually, it might help drive the point home if I gave you a few more burns."

Vanessa's shoulders fell, and she lowered her head.

"Haha! Just kidding!" Susan roared with deep-throated laughter. "I don't think it's possible to make you any *uglier*."

Stifling a relieved sigh, Vanessa raised her head and dared to glance at her mother. Susan's mood swings exhausted her. The older witch had been furious just a moment earlier, but now she brimmed with manic enthusiasm. The only thing more terrifying than an angry Susan was a happy Susan.

"Come on. Let's go." Her mother pivoted and made her way to the cabin door.

With reluctance, Vanessa obeyed. *The only way out of this mess is through it.* She trailed behind Susan, climbing the steps with intense reluctance. Her chest tightened as she prepared to reveal her scars to random witches in Beaufort.

As they crossed the yacht's deck, Susan stopped suddenly and twisted toward Front Street. "Hmmm," she growled under her breath.

"What are you waiting for?"

Susan's gaze didn't waver as she responded. "Scratch that plan. I have a better idea."

Vanessa followed her mother's line of sight to one of the shops on the other side of the street. Coastal Visions. Stevie's store.

Chapter nine

Stevie

Long past sunset, Stevie and Alice finished storing the last of the gifts in the hall closet off the foyer. Stevie had separated Vanessa's candle from the rest, still unsure of what it meant, and left it on the kitchen table.

"Well, I guess I should get going." Alice collected her jacket. "I have to get up early for church tomorrow."

Stevie yawned, exhausted from the onslaught of new information she'd acquired during her time with the elder witch. And yet, she knew she still had much more to learn. "Thanks for your help today."

"It's my pleasure, dear." The flesh surrounding Alice's eyes crinkled as she smiled. "I don't suppose I could interest you in attending church with me tomorrow morning? It might help you feel better."

The memories of her last visit to Alice's church were still fresh in her mind. Stevie crammed her hand into her pocket. Finding the chunk of sea glass, she wrapped her fingers around it. "I don't think I can make it tomorrow."

"I understand, but please, do come back sometime." Alice slipped her arms into her jacket. "I want you to see what my church is like under *normal* circumstances. They're all good people. Really."

"I know." Stevie frowned. "If I can get this situation with Susan under control, I'll come back. I promise."

Alice placed her hand on Stevie's shoulder. "Not 'if.' *When*." She gave a reassuring pat. "I know we'll figure something out. This won't go on forever."

"Okay." Stevie nodded, grateful for her use of the word 'we.' The burden of leading the witches weighed heavy on her shoulders. Too often, the responsibility left her feeling isolated, as though she alone must provide all the answers to every problem. But Alice had reminded her that she wasn't alone in this struggle. Her coven remained by her side, just as they had for her mother.

"Good night, dear. I'll see you tomorrow." Alice let herself out.

Stevie heard a light-hearted chuckle come from Dylan, who sat in the den with Charlie. She turned the lock on the front door and then made her way to the back of the house to join them.

She found them sitting side by side on the couch. Charlie balanced the open lighthouse book on his lap, and a soft, white glow blinked from its glossy page. Puzzled, Stevie tilted her head.

Dylan glanced up at her with a grin. "Check this out."

Stevie settled in next to Charlie and studied the picture on the book's page. The image featured a color photo of the lighthouse at Cape Lookout—with a very real blinking light perched atop the structure.

"Well, that's interesting." Stevie pointed to the page. "Which one of you is responsible for the light in the picture?"

Dylan shook his head. "Not me."

"Magic." A fleeting smile danced across Charlie's lips.

Stevie beamed and ruffled his curls. "That's my boy!"

Dylan pointed to some of the text on the page and read aloud. "The Cape Lookout Lighthouse is also known as The Diamond Lady. Did you know that?"

Charlie nodded and then turned the page to read about the next lighthouse.

Stevie peeked over Charlie's bowed head to catch Dylan wink at her. She loved how he fit so perfectly into their little family. She loved the special connection he had with Charlie. She loved *him*.

She so enjoyed their quiet time together that she let Charlie's bedtime slip by without a word. Stevie didn't intend to let him stay up too late, but a few extra minutes wouldn't hurt anything.

The sudden sound of dogs barking interrupted the serenity of their evening. Stevie's body tensed, and she cast a worried glance at Dylan.

"They're not close." She turned her head toward the source of the noise. "It sounds like it's coming from down the road. Maybe this has nothing to do with Ruth's strays."

A peal of sirens ripped through the night, drowning out the sound of the dogs. Stevie's eyes grew wide. "I'm going to see what's going on out there."

She rose from the sofa and hurried to the front of the house. Dylan followed close behind. She unlocked the door and swung it open, only to find a police officer walking toward her. A knot twisted in Stevie's stomach.

The young man stepped onto the porch. "Ms. Lewis?"

Breathless, she nodded. "Yes."

"I'm afraid I have some bad news."

Chapter ten

Stevie

Stevie stared at the officer. Her mouth went dry as the sirens wailed on and the dogs barked in the distance. Stepping out onto her porch, she turned east, toward the cacophony that had disturbed her peaceful evening. In a parade of flashing lights, fire trucks and police cars filed down the road and stopped amid the cluster of waterfront restaurants and shops.

An ambulance rounded the corner and joined the collection of emergency service vehicles on the street. One by one, each siren stopped with a final descending whoop, but the lights continued to flash.

The officer looked down at his feet before raising his head to meet her gaze. "Ms. Lewis, I'm sorry to tell you that there's been a fire at your store."

Stevie covered her mouth. The store had closed hours earlier, but she knew Lexi sometimes stayed after hours to work on her paintings. "Was anyone inside the building?"

The officer shook his head. "I don't know, ma'am. I came here as soon as the call came over the radio."

"But there's an ambulance…"

"They always send an ambulance to fire scenes. It doesn't necessarily mean anything," the officer explained. "I'm heading down there now. I can give you a ride if you like."

Stevie inhaled deeply as she attempted to gather her thoughts. "Yes. Thank you." She turned to Dylan. "Will you stay here with Charlie?"

"Of course." He placed his hand on the small of her back and leaned in close to her ear. "Be careful, okay?"

"I will." Stevie knew his concern extended far beyond any hazards posed by the fire.

She followed the officer to his patrol car with an undeniable tightness in her chest and remained silent until they reached the store. When Stevie emerged from the vehicle, her knees buckled at the sight before her. She gripped the door for support as she tried to make sense of the commotion. At least a dozen firefighters were on the scene, engaging in a frenzy of activity as they prepared to bring the blaze under control.

Flames licked out of the gaping hole that had once been the display window, searing the Coastal Visions sign above. Amid the roar of the fire, a sharp pop echoed in her ears as a light bulb inside the store exploded. Seconds later, the sound of glass shattering tore through the night. The crashes rang out, one by one, as framed paintings and photographs succumbed to the savage blaze. Thick smoke billowed forth, escaping through the now glassless window, and rose skyward.

Two firefighters clutched an enormous hose, directing a blast of water into the frantic flames that had overtaken her store. Six more firefighters stood nearby, dressed in full protective gear, waiting to enter the building.

Lexi.

Stevie just needed to know that Lexi was safe. She dipped her trembling hand into her pocket in search of her phone, only to discover that she'd left it at home.

She turned to the police officer who had driven her to the scene. "When will we know if anyone is in there?"

"I'll go see what I can find out for you." The officer left to go speak to one of the firefighters, leaving Stevie alone to watch her life's work burn.

The stray dogs had stopped barking, but several remained nearby. The yellow lab approached her and stood by her side. Though she'd seen the dog a few times over the last couple of days, this was the first time he had come so close to her.

Stevie stared on, motionless, as the water spray extinguished the fire inside the building. Now, she could see only one last red flame inside. It raged on, swallowing a display in the back of the store. The firefighters shifted the stream of the hose, directing it to snuff out the final blaze. Someone turned off the water, and the waiting firefighters entered the building. The surrounding air was damp and polluted with the acrid scent of burning.

Stevie stepped closer to her store, barely aware of her own feet as they shuffled across the pavement. The yellow lab stayed by her side as if she had trained him to do so.

It doesn't seem real.

The fierce blaze had charred the front of the structure beyond recognition. Her mouth fell open as she gaped at the interior, now blackened and dripping with water. A yawning, lifeless cave nestled between vibrant neighboring shops.

She had questions, so many questions.

"Stevie!"

She recognized her best friend's voice right away, and her heart soared. Stevie pressed her hand to her chest as she spun around. "You're okay!"

Teary-eyed, Lexi embraced Stevie. "I'm fine. I left hours ago." She stared at the remains of the business they had built together and shook her head. "Dylan called and told me about the fire, but I didn't expect…this."

"Me neither." A lump formed in Stevie's throat. "It's gone. Just gone."

"Do we know what caused it?"

Stevie shook her head. "I just got here myself, and they haven't told me anything. But it seems like the fire was confined to our store." She pointed to the adjoining walls of the surrounding shops. "I don't see any damage to either of those businesses."

"Well, that's good, I guess." Lexi offered a weak smile.

Stevie scanned the area searching for someone who appeared to be in charge. A small crowd of gawkers had already gathered on the boardwalk in front of the docks. Her gaze drifted beyond them and settled on the yacht that towered in the background. Spotting Susan and Vanessa on its deck, her stomach clenched.

Vanessa's hood shrouded her face, but Susan wore no such disguise. Her belligerent glare bore straight into Stevie, locked and unflinching.

Stevie refused to give the dark witch the satisfaction of her attention. She turned away, resuming her search for someone to answer her questions, and noticed the police officer talking to a man standing beside the ladder truck.

"There." Stevie pointed to him. "I bet he can tell us what happened."

Just as she took her first step toward the man, a hand clamped down on her shoulder. She whipped around to see who'd grabbed her. As soon as she saw him, she let out a relieved sigh. "Hey, Randy." She nodded to Ruth, who stood at his side.

Ruth's permanent, thin-lipped scowl intensified as she took in the sight of the burnt out store.

Deep lines stretched across Randy's forehead. "Are you girls all right?"

"We're fine." Lexi gave a slight nod. "Just a little shocked, I guess."

"The dogs told me about the fire." Ruth gestured to a gathering of strays on the nearest corner. "So we came right away."

In spite of all the weird and fantastical turns her life had taken over the last several weeks, Stevie didn't think she would ever grow accustomed to hearing Ruth say that the dogs had told her something. "Thanks for coming."

"I'll bet it was electrical." Ruth clucked. "You just never know with these older buildings. Probably lit up like kindling."

"Ruth," Randy said under his breath.

"What? I'm just pointing out the obvious." She fanned the air in front of her crinkled nose. "Whew! It really stinks out here."

"We still don't know what caused the fire. Let me see what I can find out." Stevie made her way to the man beside the ladder truck, leaving her trusted coven members to speculate amongst themselves.

The police officer glanced her way as she approached. "Ah, Ms. Lewis, this is the fire chief. He can answer your questions."

As the officer stepped away, Stevie turned to the chief. "Do you have any idea how it started?"

"Not yet." He scratched his head. "My guys haven't found any evidence to indicate an electrical problem, and there aren't any obvious signs of arson."

Stevie's back went rigid. "I see." She resisted the urge to look at Susan.

"We'll figure it out though." The fire chief held his chin high as he made the claim. "The investigation should be complete within a day or two. I'll let you know what we find."

"When can we go in there? We'd like to try to salvage whatever we can."

"You'll have to wait at least until morning, but there's nothing to salvage, ma'am. That place is a total loss. I don't know if I've ever seen a fire burn so hot that fast." The chief gestured toward the smoldering mess. "I still can't believe it didn't spread to the other stores."

Stevie thanked him and returned to Lexi, Ruth, and Randy. She filled them in on the little information she'd acquired but stopped short of sharing her theory with them.

"That's weird." Lexi crossed her arms.

"I'm sure sorry this happened, girls." Randy touched Stevie's elbow. "Let me know if there's anything I can do to help."

Stevie nodded. "Thanks, Randy."

Ruth shrugged and let her hands slap against her thighs. "I guess there's nothing more we can do here tonight." Her hard expression softened slightly, and she leaned in close to Stevie. "You call us if you need us, okay?"

"I will."

Ruth bent over with a grunt and patted the yellow lab's head. "You're a good boy."

As the yellow lab wagged his tail in reply, Stevie thought she saw a hint of a rare smile tug on Ruth's lips.

Randy and Ruth left, but the dog stayed by Stevie's side while firefighters began to emerge from the ashes within the store and return to the fire trucks. Two men worked to put away the hose while a few took a quick break.

Stevie caught snippets of their conversations.

"Can't believe it didn't spread."

"That was the *hottest* fire I've ever seen. Crazy!"

She tilted her head, unable to fathom what constituted extreme heat to the brave men and women who worked among flames.

A single firefighter in full protective gear stepped out of the store and made his way toward Stevie. As he approached, the yellow lab at her feet let out a low growl and moved to stand in front of her. The man stopped when he reached Stevie and Lexi, launching the dog into a furious barking fit.

The firefighter raised his visor and leaned down toward the dog. "Hush!"

Stevie flinched at the man's tone, but she couldn't deny it was effective. The yellow lab stopped barking and returned to Stevie's side with a whimper.

"Any news?" Stevie asked, hopeful that the firefighter had uncovered the source of the blaze.

"Nope." The man brushed away a smudge of soot on the cuff of his thick coat. "They're never going to figure out what caused this fire."

His harsh words set Stevie aback. "What makes you say that?"

"Because I did it."

Chapter eleven

Stevie

Flashing lights from the patrol car reflected on the firefighter's hard helmet. "I wouldn't have had to do this if you'd renounced your role as queen." His lip curled as he leaned in closer to Stevie. "But you just *had* to follow in mommy's footsteps, didn't you?"

Stevie heartbeat thundered in her ears. She turned away from him to steal a quick glance at the yacht. Only Vanessa stood on its deck now.

The firefighter's expression pinched in annoyance. "That's right; it's me." His face began to morph, bones flowing under rubbery skin.

Stevie watched in horror as his masculine features became more delicate. His angular jaw and thick brows faded away, revealing high cheekbones, arched eyebrows, and a narrow chin. Only the malevolent grin remained.

The yellow lab suddenly ran off, issuing frantic barks. Stevie had no doubt he'd gone to get Ruth. She also knew there was nothing Ruth could do to save her from Susan.

Firefighters continued their bustle of activity, unaware of Susan's metamorphosis. Still wearing the helmet and the cumbersome gear, the dark witch had drawn no attention to herself.

"It's time we put an end to the idea that you're the *queen*." Susan snarled. "I've allowed this silliness to go on long enough."

Stevie clenched her jaw as the image of her mother's lifeless body flashed in her mind.

Lexi let out a low hiss. "What do you want, Susan?" Her fist rose slowly, and a pale glow began to emanate from her folded fingers.

Stevie grabbed Lexi's arm, forcing her to lower her hand. "Not here."

Susan's eyes brightened with amusement as she watched Stevie restrain Lexi. "I want to show the others who's really in charge now. They're all so committed to the ridiculous notion that only one family can lead them. They just need to see what I can do. Of course, they also need to know about the amulet and how *your* family hid it from them all these years."

Stevie kept her eyes locked on Susan, well aware of the danger the dark witch posed to the innocent residents and first responders whom she'd drawn out by starting the fire in Coastal Visions. "Exactly how do you plan to show them this?"

"Let's meet at the Cape. Next Saturday, under the full moon." Susan smirked. "I want you to bring *all* of the witches in town, not just your little coven."

Stevie's cheeks grew hot with rage. "I'm not going to put my people at risk just so you can put on a magic show."

"I won't hurt *my* people." Susan rested her hand on over her heart as though Stevie's statement had offended her. "I only want them there as witnesses. As long as they behave themselves, they'll be fine. I can't say the same for you…but I suspect you knew that already."

"No." Stevie's hands balled into tight fists. "I won't do that."

"It's cute that you think I'm asking." Susan cackled. "Let me put it a different way. You *will* show up at the Cape next Saturday with the other witches, or I will *kill* your son."

Stevie's reply turned to stone in her throat as her knees threatened to fail her. She had no doubt that the dark witch would follow through with her threat.

"I believe I've made myself clear." Without further discussion, Susan whirled around and strolled away.

"What are we going to do?" Lexi spoke in a barely audible whisper, her voice tinged with panic.

Heavy footsteps pounded against the pavement behind them. Stevie jerked her head toward the sound to find Ruth and Randy hurrying in her direction with the yellow lab leading the way. All three were panting from the effort of rushing to get back to her.

"What's going on? The dog..." Ruth hunched forward, gasping for air.

"It was Susan." Lexi pursed her lips. "She just challenged Stevie to a public standoff. She wants to show off her power in front of *all* the witches." She crossed her arms and glowered, abandoning her initial fear to reveal the anger that had settled in its place.

Stevie's wary gaze flicked back to the yacht, where Vanessa still stood alone on the deck. She'd offered no warnings this time. Not even for Charlie's sake.

Squaring her shoulders, Stevie faced Ruth, Randy, and Lexi. "We'll have a coven meeting tomorrow to discuss our options." She hoped that she would somehow come up with a strategy to discuss by then. As it stood, she saw no way out of the predicament.

"Let's get you both out of here." Randy placed his hand on Stevie's shoulder. "I'll give you a ride home."

Stevie waved away the offer. "I'm okay. I'll just walk home. I could use the time to think."

Ruth shook her head. "Absolutely not! What if Susan comes back?"

An officer stretched police tape across the front of the shop as the fire truck engines roared to life, announcing their imminent departure.

Stevie stared into the smoky blackness that had swallowed the store she loved so much. "She won't hurt me now. She needs me alive so she can kill me at the Cape."

Without another word, Stevie began plodding toward her home. The yellow lab's claws clicked against the sidewalk as he trailed behind her. Her mind raced, desperately seeking a solution. She didn't know what show of force Susan had planned, so she couldn't begin to form a defensive plan.

Maybe it's time to play offense. The thought did little to bolster her spirits. She still had no strategy. No plan. No hope.

The yellow lab followed her all the way to her yard, stopping just outside her gate. Stevie bent down to pat his back, and her fingers bumped against the sharp outlines of his ribs. With quick steps, she went inside her house and hustled straight to the kitchen. She wasn't in the habit of feeding strays, but this one had begun to grow on her. She opened the refrigerator in search of leftovers to feed the skinny dog. Seeing that the ham her father had given her remained in ample supply, she pulled it out and set it on the counter.

Stevie heard Dylan's footsteps in the hallway as he made his way from the den to the kitchen. She gulped, imagining how he'd react to the news of Susan's ultimatum.

The plain ivory pillar that she'd left on the table earlier caught her eye. Vanessa's gift, a supposed pledge of loyalty.

Bullshit. Stevie snatched the candle from the table and threw it in the garbage can.

She returned to her work of preparing a plate for the stray dog who'd stayed by her side during the night's ordeal. Whatever that poor dog had been through in his life, he would at least eat well tonight.

Chapter twelve

Stevie

The welcome scent of frying bacon wafted up the staircase and into Stevie's bedroom on Sunday morning. After pulling on a pair of well-worn jeans and a long sleeve t-shirt, she stole a quick glimpse of herself in the mirror to find dark circles under her eyes. She sighed, imagining the multistep beauty regimen that Lexi would employ to hide the evidence of a poor night's sleep.

She gathered her hair and swept it back into a ponytail. *Good enough.*

Stevie padded downstairs and found Dylan in the kitchen, scrambling eggs in a frying pan while the bacon cooled on a plate beside the stove.

He glanced up as she entered the room but didn't greet her with his usual warm smile. "I don't suppose you've changed your mind since last night."

Stevie propped her hand on her hip. "She'll come for Charlie if I don't go through with it. I *have* to face her at the Cape."

Deep creases furrowed across his forehead. "We both know how that will end."

"There's no other way."

Dylan remained quiet for a long moment while he stirred the eggs in the pan. "Breakfast is almost ready." He didn't look at her.

"Okay, I'll go get Charlie."

She made her way to the den and found her son putting the final touches on an elaborate Lincoln Log house he'd set up on the coffee table.

Stevie marveled at his work, which displayed a level of skill far beyond that of most five-year-olds. Though she'd spared him the details of the current threat, she knew he had already detected the tension in the house. His deep frown and furrowed brow betrayed his concern, a level of worry that would be too much to bear for many adults. While he worked, he watched a puppet-themed television show designed for toddlers. Between autism and his unusual gift, Charlie seemed to be every age at once.

Stevie drew in a deep breath, trying to ease the tightness in her chest. "This is really great, Charlie." She gestured toward the cabin.

He didn't respond. Instead, he watched the characters who danced in primary shades of color on the television screen.

"Breakfast is ready. Are you hungry?"

He nodded and began to walk past Stevie, heading toward the kitchen.

"Charlie, wait," she said. More than anything, she wanted to tell him that everything would be okay. She wished she could tell him that there was nothing to worry about, but she couldn't bring herself to lie to him.

When he looked her way, she offered the biggest smile she could muster before kneeling down to meet his fleeting glance.

She ruffled his blond curls and planted a kiss on his forehead. "I love you."

Together, they walked down the hall and joined Dylan at the kitchen table. Stevie's appetite remained elusive as she poked at her breakfast with her fork, punctuating the awkward silence with clinks and scrapes. She managed to eat only a couple of bites before giving up and sipping her coffee instead.

She glanced at Charlie. *I have to prepare him...for life without me.* Her stomach clenched tighter.

"Please try to eat." Dylan raised a piece of bacon to his mouth. "You need your strength."

"I can't." Her voice cracked with emotion.

Every single day since Charlie had received his autism diagnosis, she'd worried about what would happen to him after she died. But those concerns had all been centered on his *adult* life. Would he be able to take care of himself? Would he have friends? Would he be happy? These were the worries that had stolen her sleep so often over the last few years. They haunted her without mercy, even though she expected to have several more decades with him. Always, she soothed herself with the hope that she'd have ample time to prepare him for a life without her.

But now, she didn't have decades of life left with him. She only had a few days.

Charlie was not yet the man she expected to leave behind someday. He was just a little boy. She still had so much more to teach him.

Her throat constricted as hot tears threatened to fall. Keeping her head down, she excused herself from the table and went upstairs to her bedroom.

Stevie sat on the edge of her bed, collecting her thoughts. It would be easy to give in to the onslaught of tears, to hide under the covers and wail against the unfairness of it all. But she wouldn't do that. She wasn't ready to give up. Not today.

She listened to Dylan's heavy footsteps on the stairs and then to the creak of the floorboards in the hall as he made his way to her bedroom.

He came to stand in the doorway and tilted his head. "Are you okay, Stevie?"

"I'm fine."

He joined her on the bed and wrapped his arm around her, pulling her toward him. She rested her head against his chest, blinking back another flood of tears as she settled into his embrace. They had so little time left together.

He rubbed her arm with a gentle stroke. "Let's take my new boat out for a spin today. We could all use the fresh air."

Stevie bit her lip, considering the invitation. She'd love nothing more than to be on the water with Dylan and Charlie. But she had work to do.

"That sounds great, but I have to take care of some things related to the store fire." She pulled away but did not meet his gaze. "I'm sure there will be a ton of insurance paperwork to deal with. Why don't you take Charlie? He'd enjoy a boat ride."

Dylan's expression hardened. "I don't like leaving you here alone."

"I'll be fine—at least until Saturday." Stevie offered a sad smile. "Besides, the coven members are always checking on me. I'm sure I won't be alone for long."

Stevie waved from her front porch as Dylan and Charlie coasted away in the sleek new speedboat. She watched them head east until the vessel shrunk to a tiny red dot in the distance. As soon as they moved out of sight, she hurried across the street toward her skiff.

The skinny, yellow lab napped on the edge of the dock. He raised his head and thumped his tail as she approached.

Stevie stopped to pet him, giving him a good scratch behind the ears. "Wish I had more time, buddy. But there's something I have to take care of."

She rose and stepped into her little boat. The stray dog jumped in behind her, but she didn't protest. Together, they motored out to the middle of Taylor's Creek where she and Dylan had sunk the safe the night of the binding ritual.

Alice and Dylan's concerns about Vanessa's magic weighed heavy on her mind. *But it's my only viable option.*

If Susan succeeding in killing her on Saturday, Charlie would be left without a mother, and her people would be left without a true queen. There would be no one to protect them from the dark witch's wrath. If Stevie wanted any chance, however small, of defeating her, she needed more magic—Vanessa's magic.

Going behind Dylan's back to retrieve the safe left her with a gnawing sense of guilt. She brushed it aside, reminding herself that she had to do whatever it took to defeat Susan. It wasn't fear of his anger or disappointment that led her to take on this task in secrecy. Her actions were born from a desire to protect her people. In this case, she only wanted to spare Alice and Dylan, as well as the rest of the coven, the burden of unnecessary worry.

Her thoughts drifted to Charlotte, Hannah, and Catherine, the first witches to live in Beaufort. Trapped aboard Blackbeard's *Queen Anne's Revenge*, they too had faced what seemed like an impossible situation. Stevie recalled the historic visions she had witnessed on the night of her coven initiation. Those fearless women had managed to execute a creative plan to secure their escape from the pirate ship—and keep their magic a secret in the process.

They'd worked together to accomplish their goal. Pooling their considerable power, they had constructed an enormous sandbar to block the vessel's path. With another burst of concentrated magic, they sent a gust of wind to propel the ship straight into it—grounding the *Queen Anne's Revenge* forever. In the chaos that ensued, they'd made their way to safety.

Stevie pressed her lips together. Over the centuries, due to the need for secrecy, witches had stopped working together the way they'd done so long ago. Her coven represented only a small fraction of the witch population in Beaufort. All of the others were solitary practitioners.

What might they accomplish if they all worked together? Could their combined effort be enough to destroy Susan? *Maybe.*

She cast a furtive glance back toward Front Street where Vanessa's floating palace towered over all of the other boats at the dock. From her low location on Taylor's Creek, Stevie didn't have a clear view of the yacht's deck, and its tinted windows made it impossible for her to see if anyone watched her from inside the vessel.

Stevie didn't know when she'd have another moment alone. She had to get the safe now, while she had the chance. Still, she felt exposed in the late morning sun.

Taking care to use her magic as inconspicuously as possible, she envisioned the safe as it had appeared the night she and Dylan had dropped it into the water—about twelve inches wide and steel gray, with a combination lock. She closed her eyes. This time, she pictured it at the bottom of the creek, nestled in the sand. She visualized it rising up through the calm water, silt falling away from it in drifting strands. Higher and higher it rose, from the darkened depths, toward the light above until it breached the surface.

Stevie opened her eyes to scan the water around her skiff and located the safe right away, off to her right, just out of reach. Once again, she focused her magic on it, this time allowing it to float just beneath the rippling waves while she drew it toward her. When it was finally within reach, she leaned over the edge and heaved it on board. It struck the bottom of her boat with a thud and a spray of water droplets.

"There! We did it." Stevie grinned at the yellow lab who replied with an enthusiastic tail wag.

Anxious to get back inside and absorb Vanessa powers before Dylan came back, she motored across the creek and secured her skiff at her dock. She grabbed a towel from under one of the seats and wiped away the remaining water from the safe.

Using both arms, she lifted it and placed it on her dock before climbing out of her boat. Grateful that it wasn't heavier than it was, she hauled the safe back across the street to her house. The stray dog trailed behind her all the way up the dock and across the street. He stopped when he reached the bottom of her porch steps.

With her hands full, Stevie had to use her magic to open the door to her house. As it swung open, she glanced back at the yellow lab. "I'll bring some more ham out for you, buddy."

Kicking the door closed behind her, she stepped into her dining room and lowered the safe onto the table. Despite the fact that it had been submerged in salt water for several weeks, it remained in excellent condition. She ran her hand across its smooth top and wondered if her mother had placed some sort of protective spell on it before giving it to Dylan to sink.

Stevie focused on the combination lock, willing it to spin. When the dial rotated, her heart began to race with anticipation—and a touch of fear.

The rumble of a car engine interrupted her focus, halting her magic. She peeked through the window and saw a champagne colored Buick pull up in front of her house. Ruth and Randy had come to check on her.

She wrapped her arms around the safe and hustled toward the hall closet. With a concentrated burst of magic, she swung its door open only to find that all of the shelves were already full, stocked with the gifts left by loyal witches.

Stevie heard her visitors' voices grow louder as they approached the house. Squatting down, she shoved the safe along the floor until it reached the back corner of the closet.

She closed the door and slumped against it. *I hate being sneaky.*

The doorbell rang. Though it wasn't unexpected, she jumped at the sound. Stevie took in a deep breath in an attempt to settle her frazzled nerves and then wiped the beads of sweat from her brow before she answered the door.

Chapter Thirteen

Vanessa

On Sunday morning, Vanessa stood on the deck of her yacht, watching a small herd of wild horses walk along Carrot Island's sandy shore. She pulled her hood as far forward as it would go, shielding her burns from the sun's damaging rays and—with any luck—protecting herself from Susan's scrutiny. Sometimes, Vanessa viewed her hood as her refuge. But more often than not, it felt like a prison.

In just six days, everything would change. There'd be no coven, no Stevie, and Susan would be the new queen. She intended to play her part in order to earn favor with her mother. Maybe then she'd get her magic back.

She bit her lip. *Maybe.*

She glanced back at her mother, who lounged on the opposite side of the yacht's deck. Susan always seemed to prefer the view of Front Street. Now, she had the added benefit of ogling the charred remains of Stevie's store, which was nothing more than a vacant black hollow. An eye burnt out with a firebrand.

Surveying her kingdom with an imperious air, Susan *looked* regal enough. Perhaps she was destined to be the queen after all.

"It won't be long now." Susan's smug grin confirmed her total confidence in her plan.

"It seems unlikely that the witches will welcome you as their queen if they watch you kill Stevie, and surely no one would want the little boy to be hurt." Vanessa traced her finger along the deck's railing.

"Just you wait and see." Susan nodded in agreement with herself. "If everything goes perfectly—and it will—*I* won't be the one who does the killing."

Vanessa's eyebrow arched. "How do you plan to do that?"

"I can't show you now. Later, though, I'll let you in on my surprise." She watched the pedestrians who wandered along the boardwalk. "I wonder if Stevie has called for an emergency coven meeting yet? Surely, she'll want to get all of those nitwits together to discuss her impending demise."

Susan reached for her binoculars and raised them to her eyes, focusing on Stevie's house. In an instant, she bolted straight up and tilted her head. "Well, I didn't expect *that*." She let out a low hiss of surprise.

Curious, Vanessa crossed to the other side of the deck to see what had captured her mother's attention. "What's happening?"

Susan held the binoculars up for Vanessa to take. "Here. See for yourself."

Vanessa accepted the binoculars without a word and peered through them. She could only see the roof of one of the waterfront buildings and some of the trees that lined Front Street. She frowned, frustrated. "I can't see anything." She lowered the binoculars.

Susan snickered. "Oh, silly me! I forgot you lost your magic." She gave a quick wave of her hand. "There, now try again."

Vanessa's lip curled into a sneer. Her mother never missed an opportunity to remind her of her inadequacies. She raised the binoculars and stared through the lenses once more.

Now, she had a clear view of Stevie walking toward her porch. A skinny yellow dog followed behind her, wagging his tail. "She's carrying something. It looks heavy."

Susan smirked. "Do you know what it is?"

"No." Vanessa shook her head as she set the binoculars on the table.

"That's the safe they locked your magic in."

Vanessa met her mother's piercing gaze, dumbfounded. "Why would she carry it inside?"

"Who knows?" Susan shrugged. "Maybe she intends to absorb your powers to make herself stronger. Like that would help." She snorted.

My magic. Overcome with dizziness, Vanessa gripped the railing of the deck, turning her knuckles white.

Chapter fourteen

Stevie

On Sunday afternoon, Stevie stood with Ruth on her front porch as black clouds rolled over Beaufort. The other coven members had just arrived and were waiting inside the house. But her worry for the stray yellow lab forced her to delay the start of their meeting.

"Looks like this is going to be a bad storm. I just want to make sure he's safe."

Ruth waved away Stevie's concern. "These strays know how to ride out a shower. He'll be fine, I'm sure."

Stevie scanned the area, first looking toward her dock across the street and then glancing up and down the length of Front Street. She didn't see the dog anywhere. Her shoulders dropped. "You're probably right, but I would feel better knowing he's safe and dry."

Ruth barked a chuckle. "So you're a dog owner now, huh?"

"No." Stevie shook her head. "Definitely not. I don't have time for a pet."

"Right." Ruth stretched the word as she spoke it. "He's probably close by. Do you want me to call him?"

The temperature plummeted as a swift wind picked up, scattering leaves from the southern live oak trees that dotted her yard. Stevie shuddered and rubbed her arms to warm herself. "Yes. Please."

Ruth stood still and quiet for a long moment as she used her magic to call for the stray dog. When she completed her task, a hint of a smile flashed across her thin lips. "He's on his way."

Stevie heard rustling in the bush off the left side of her porch as the yellow lab emerged from his hiding place. Making his way to the bottom of the porch steps, he wagged his tail when he saw her.

"He likes you." Ruth jerked her head toward the dog.

Stevie patted her thighs. "Come here, buddy."

He made his way up the porch steps as fat raindrops began to fall from the sky. They hurtled down faster and faster, each one smacking against the ground with an undignified plop. Relieved to have the stray under the porch roof, Stevie scratched his head. "Come on inside." She opened her front door.

The dog didn't move.

"He wants to stay out here," Ruth explained. "He likes to be able to keep an eye on things."

"He's still protecting me?"

"And Charlie." Ruth nodded. "He seems to have developed an attachment to both of you."

Stevie stepped closer to the dog and knelt down beside him. She ran her hands across his dirty coat, feeling the ridges of ribs along his side. "Does he have a name?"

Ruth shook her head. "This one has always been a stray. No one's ever given him a name, but he likes it when you call him buddy."

"Buddy it is," Stevie said as she stood up. "If he's going to stay out here, I want to get him a blanket and some food. After that, we'll start the meeting."

Ruth followed Stevie inside. "Okay, I'll let the others know."

Stevie couldn't deny that she felt a little silly worrying about a stray animal in light of all that was going on. She might not be able to stop Susan's path of chaos and destruction, but it was well within her power to help a dog feel more comfortable, even if only for a little while.

With Buddy settled on the front porch, she joined the coven members in the kitchen. Lexi, Deborah, Alice, and Ruth had all taken seats at the tile-topped table. Randy and Dylan stood nearby. Charlie was nestled in Lexi's lap, sharing pictures from his lighthouse book with her.

Deborah worked at a feverish pace on her seemingly endless spell blanket, now adding rows of white yarn to the creation. Stevie knew that color represented protection. Now, she could count yarn among her arsenal of magical protections. *Why not?* If the stray dogs, random rocks, and a salt circle weren't enough to save her from Susan, it was good to know that this blanket had her back.

She pinched the bridge of her nose and sighed.

Lexi squealed with delight as the light in the photo of Cape Lookout began to blink. Charlie beamed at her reaction.

"I hate to break up the fun, but it's time for the grownups to talk," Stevie said to Charlie. "Will you go play in your room for a little while?"

He nodded and slid off Lexi's lap, leaving his book behind on the table. Stevie waited until he was out of earshot to speak. They had plenty to discuss, and none of it was appropriate for him to hear. She listened as his footsteps traveled up the staircase and onto the second floor.

Stevie drew in a deep breath as she sought the words she needed to say. Dylan came to stand by her side, grabbed her hand, and gave it a quick squeeze before releasing it.

Dreading the discussion that would follow, Stevie forced herself to speak. "I'm sure you've all heard by now that I agreed to meet Susan at the Cape on Saturday night. I'm supposed to bring all of the solitary witches from town as well." She lowered her voice. "If I don't show up, *or* if I fail to bring the other witches, she'll—" She couldn't bring herself to utter it the rest of the sentence.

Dylan reached for her hand again. "They know, Stevie."

The coven members' grim expressions reflected everything she knew to be true. She had to confront Susan—and she wouldn't survive the encounter.

"I'm not afraid to die, but I'm not willing to leave my people in Susan's hands. Who knows what she might do to you and to…" She paused as her throat tightened. "Charlie."

"We'll all fight!" Lexi pounded her fist against the table. "We'll do whatever it takes to stop her."

"I know you want to protect me, but we all saw what happened to my mother. Our combined efforts aren't nearly enough to stop Susan." Stevie placed her hand on Lexi's shoulder. "But I do have an idea—"

Ruth hunched forward in her chair. "Well don't keep us waiting. Spit it out!"

Stevie cleared her throat. "I know our magic wasn't enough to stop Susan, but what if *all* the witches helped?"

Lexi's eyes lit up. "Yes! If they all come, we'll have *hundreds* of witches on our side. Surely that's enough to stop her."

Ruth sank back in her chair with a groan.

"No, dear." Alice shook her head. "I'm afraid that still won't be enough."

"Why not?" Stevie asked.

Alice leaned forward, resting her arms on the table. "Your grandmother once told me that the amulet grants the queen the power of a thousand witches. I'm not sure if we're meant to take that literally. It could be more, for all we know."

"Oh." Stevie's shoulders slumped. She couldn't ask her people to help knowing they had no chance of beating Susan. *It would be a death sentence for all of them.* Stepping away from the table, she glanced at Dylan. His dark eyes reflected the same hopelessness that gripped her heart.

She shifted her attention to the window, as if the answer to her problems lay somewhere beyond its glass pane. A fierce wind howled as a flash of lightning illuminated the gloomy sky.

A jolt of realization coursed through Stevie, and she whirled back around. "Only three witches settled in Beaufort in 1718. Lucia's group had dozens more. How can we find where they settled?"

Deborah looked up from her knitting. "Patricia tried to locate the others years ago. She wasn't able to find them."

"I know your grandmother tried as well," Alice said. "I would bet many other queens have done the same."

"I find that hard to believe." Stevie pursed her lips. "Especially since they had the power of the amulet to help them."

Randy uncrossed his arms and straightened his shoulders. "What if Lucia put some sort of blocking spell in the amulet. We know she told Charlotte not to try to find her. What if she made it *impossible* for her daughter to do so?"

The room fell silent as the coven members processed Randy's theory. It made sense to Stevie. The two groups had somehow remained separate for three centuries. That couldn't have been an accident. It had to be by design.

Dylan cocked his head. "Randy might be onto something, Stevie. I think we should try to find them ourselves since we don't have the amulet to stop us."

Stevie's pulse quickened as she considered the new strategy. "Yes! Let's do it."

"I remember the spell Patricia used for this before." Deborah shoved her knitting needles back into her bag. "We're going to need a map."

"I have one in the Buick." Randy stepped toward the kitchen doorway. "I'll go get it."

Chapter Fifteen

Vanessa

Heavy rain thrummed against the fiberglass roof of Vanessa's yacht. Any other time, she would have enjoyed the sounds of a raging storm. But being cooped up in the cabin while Susan completed her latest rant was anything but fun.

"I'll make them pay…" Her mother droned on.

Vanessa sank back against the couch cushions and watched the storm through the window. A brilliant, jagged bolt of white lightning flashed across the sky and dipped into Taylor's Creek before it disappeared. A clap of thunder soon followed, punctuating the squall-fueled symphony and rattling the yacht's windows.

"Amulet….power…queen."

Blah, blah, blah. Vanessa crossed her arms. She'd rather listen to the rain than hear her mother rehash the same venomous monologue for the millionth time.

Another flash of lightning zipped across the sky. Pulsing, electric, illuminating. *Just like when Charlie touched my arm.* She closed her eyes, remembering his visit to her hospital room. After all she'd subjected him to, she had expected him to hurt her. Instead, he'd used his strange gift to wash away the anger that had defined her for so long. It had only lasted a moment—just long enough to give her a glimpse of another way of being—a life apart from her mother's violence, greed, and retribution. But with Susan's rise to power an imminent certainty, Vanessa knew she'd never have the opportunity to live in the light that Charlie had shown her.

Just as well. It's not who I am anyway.

Vanessa opened her eyes to find her mother standing stock still before her. Her stomach clenched. She hadn't noticed that Susan had completed her diatribe.

Susan gripped the stem of her martini glass. "Am I *boring* you?"

Vanessa sat up straighter on the couch and cleared her throat. "I'm sorry. I was just wondering how you planned to take care of Stevie. You said you would tell me the plan."

Susan took a generous swig of her drink and studied her for a long, uncomfortable moment. "I suppose it *is* time to let you in on my little surprise." She set her glass on the coffee table.

Catching the gleam in Susan's eye, icy fingers danced up Vanessa's spine. Whatever her mother had planned was sure to be devastating to the coven.

"You said you weren't going to be the one to kill Stevie and—" Vanessa paused, unwilling to utter his name, "the boy."

"Right!" Susan grinned. "That's because I'm bringing some friends to help."

Vanessa tilted her head, baffled. Susan had no friends that she knew of.

"Now watch." The amulet that hung from her neck began to glow as Susan raised her arms. She outlined an oval in the air before her. It stood about two feet tall and hovered well above the ground, blocking Vanessa's view of her mother's face. Within the shape, a ribbon of lavender light traveled across the center of the space as though it were coasting on a meandering wave. It curved and twisted, filling much of the available area. The pastel thread remained in motion, throbbing, though it never left the two-dimensional floating plane.

Mesmerized by the sight, Vanessa's breath slowed, and the tightness in her stomach relaxed. The simple organic beauty of the lavender hue was as tranquil as it was puzzling.

Suddenly, a ribbon of black burst into the oblong frame. Vanessa jumped back in surprise. As it snaked in and around its lavender counterpart, her body tensed. Over and under it slithered until it had filled all of the remaining space within the shape, displacing her tranquility with dread.

The ribbons of light and dark were entirely interwoven yet remained separate from one another. Though their travels within the oval appeared complete, they both continued to move in and around each other as if teeming with life yearning to burst forth.

"What is it, Mother?"

Susan stepped out from behind her hovering creation, beaming with pride. "*This* is the veil to the afterlife."

Vanessa's mouth fell open. Whatever "friends" her mother planned to have at her side must be coming from beyond the veil.

A subtle glow still emanated from the amulet as Susan took a moment to admire her own handiwork. "In ancient times, our queens routinely opened this portal to visit with their deceased loved ones. However, recent generations of queens have forbidden the practice. Since modern witches lack the pure, undiluted magic of our ancestors, we no longer possess the strength to keep the dark souls restrained when we allow light souls to cross over to our side."

Susan patted the amethyst. "But we don't have to worry about that." She laughed, her eyes bright with excitement. "It's the *dark souls* I want." She traced the black ribbon with her index finger. "Somewhere within this thread, there's a particularly nasty devil who will be more than happy to help me."

"Who?" Vanessa's voice sounded hollow in the presence of both the veil and the queen who now sought to rule the dead as well as the living.

"There's not enough room on this boat for me to show you." Susan glanced over her shoulder at Vanessa. "So you get to be as surprised as everyone else on Saturday." She spoke as if she were awarding her daughter a long-awaited gift.

Susan clapped her hands together below her waist and then raised them above her head, reversing the motion she had originally made to open the portal. The oval disappeared, taking the ribbons of lavender and black along with it. "I'll have plenty of help. If any of the witches attempt to cross me, I'll put them down instantly."

Vanessa's heart raced. Stevie didn't stand a chance. Neither did the kid.

After providing Susan with sufficient kudos for her ingenious plan, she left the living area for the quiet comfort of her own quarters. She entered her room and closed the door behind her.

She took in the sight of the candleholder that now sat empty on her nightstand. Frustrated with her mother, she'd left the ivory pillar on Stevie's porch only the day before and already regretted doing it. She couldn't pledge her loyalty to a queen who would surely be defeated.

Chapter sixteen

Stevie

Night had begun to fall on Beaufort as Randy stood in Stevie's kitchen, unfolding a road map of the United States. He pushed Charlie's lighthouse book out of the way and then laid the map on Stevie's kitchen table. Raindrops had dotted the thin paper when he carried it from his car, but it was in otherwise perfect condition. Interstates and highways showed as red lines crossing over the black borders separating the lower forty-eight states. Printed names of cities and small towns peppered the entire page.

Lexi let out a low whistle. "I don't remember the last time I used a paper map."

Stevie nodded. "Same here." She turned to Deborah. "What else do we need?"

"Gemstones. Specifically, we'll need four pieces of clear quartz to amplify the spell." Deborah counted the items off on her fingers. "And a smooth amethyst would work well as a pointer, if you have one."

"No problem." Alice stepped forward. "Stevie received plenty of stones as gifts from the other witches. I'll go get them from the closet. I'll grab a candle too."

The last thing Stevie wanted was to have Alice rummage through the closet. "I'll get them." She hurried out of the kitchen before anyone had a chance to reply.

Finding the other witches could help them gain an advantage against Susan. But Stevie knew that even if they could find the others, there was no guarantee they would fight on her behalf.

When she opened the hall closet door, she spotted the small safe she'd stowed in the corner. *My backup plan.* The desperate, last-ditch effort to save her people could result in either their salvation or her own utter destruction. Anything was possible with untested magic. Nevertheless, she intended to absorb Vanessa's powers as soon as she had a minute alone.

Shaking off her concerns, Stevie plucked an old camera box containing the gemstones from the shelf and tucked it under her arm. Then she scanned the shelves in search of a plain candle. She reached for one that was similar to the ivory pillar that Vanessa had left for her, only this one had come from a *loyal* witch. She grabbed it and pushed the closet door closed with her hip before hurrying back to the kitchen.

Stevie set the box on the table and placed the candle just to the right of the map. She sorted through the stones in search of the ones she needed. Once she collected them all, she turned to Deborah for guidance.

Following her instructions, Stevie placed a piece of clear quartz on each corner of the roadmap. She cupped the small amethyst and considered where to place it for the purpose of their magical workings.

"My mother told me that Lucia had planned to find another home among the colonists." Stevie placed the purple gemstone on the middle of the Eastern Seaboard.

"That's right, dear." Alice nodded. "Good choice."

"Are you ready to lead us in this spell?" Deborah asked.

"I don't know the words." Stevie's chest tightened. "Maybe you should do it."

Deborah shook her head. "It's really better if the queen leads."

Lexi offered an encouraging smile. "You can do this."

"Don't worry about the words, my dear. Just speak from your heart. They don't even have to rhyme." Alice grinned. "Though, I must admit, it's a nice touch."

In Stevie's limited experience with group spells, she had already discerned that there was no single right way to achieve the goal. She considered the night the coven members had worked together to bind Vanessa's powers and how they had all focused on one intention. She thought about how Charlotte, Catherine, and Hannah combined their powers on the *Queen Anne's Revenge*. In both cases, the techniques had differed among the queens, but each one had succeeded in harnessing the power of multiple witches.

Lexi switched off the kitchen light, plunging the coven into darkness. Then, without the aid of a lighter or a match, she ignited the wick on the candle, replacing the gloom with a dim, flickering glow that made their shadows dance on the walls.

A sudden flash of lightning illuminated the room, revealing to Stevie that all eyes were now on her.

"Okay." She took in a deep breath.

I can do this.

"Please stand and join hands." Stevie extended her hands, grasping Dylan's with her left and Lexi's with her right.

She focused on the amethyst resting on the map. "We seek to make our people one, lest the kingdom come undone." Her voice echoed weak in her own ears as it broke through the silence of the group. She stifled a cringe, feeling rather silly about reciting a rhyme she'd just made up on the spot.

I can't worry about that now. I have to focus.

"Show us where Lucia went. Know that there is no harm meant." Her voice grew stronger as the magic of the coven came alive.

Dylan squeezed her hand in approval.

In unison, the coven repeated her words. "Show us where Lucia went. Know that there is no harm meant."

A swell of energy soared through Stevie as their combined powers coalesced in the circle created by their outstretched arms. Bands of white light emanated from each witch, embracing the purple stone on the map.

"Show us where Lucia went. Know that there is no harm meant." Stevie's voice rose over the others as she led them in the chant.

Her heart raced as her own searing magic flowed through her. It electrified her body and poured out over the map. The amethyst began to move, rocking and tapping against the map as if it were unwilling to give up its secrets.

The chant continued. "Show us where Lucia went. Know that there is no harm meant."

The wobbling gemstone broke away from its spot on the East Coast and spun in place over the Atlantic Ocean, twirling with increasing speed. It began to spiral, turning outward over and over again, expanding its orbit to encompass the full map. Faster it went, until it was nothing more than a lavender blur against the colorful paper.

"Show us where Lucia went. Know that there is no harm meant."

The combined power of the coven members flowed through Stevie. They shared a sole magical intention, uniting their focus in one purpose.

In a final flash of movement, the amethyst zipped back to its original place on the Eastern Seaboard and came to a dead stop. The map's edges began to curl, folding in on itself. The sound of crumpling paper cut through the stunned silence of the witches as the map continued to crush itself into a tight ball.

As the magic in the room evaporated, so did Stevie's hope. Her shoulders slumped as she released her hold on Lexi's and Dylan's hands.

"What the hell?" Lexi turned on the overhead light and blew out the candle.

Deborah sighed. "That's the same thing that happened when Patricia tried it."

Randy reached forward and picked up the crumpled remains of his map. "Well, whatever spell is blocking us from locating the others, it's not just in the amulet. There's serious magic at play here."

Alice nodded. "Lucia really didn't want her group to be found."

Stevie, frustrated by the failure of her first group spell, stepped away from the table. Her mind raced. There *had* to be a way to connect with the others. She began to pace the length of the kitchen as the wind howled outside.

Randy pried open the knot of paper and pulled the amethyst from its center. He tossed the ruined map into the trashcan.

A flash of lightning lit up the window and faded away. Stevie gasped as a new thought occurred to her. "If we can't find them, maybe we could help *them* find *us*."

"How can we draw their attention without letting the rest of the world know about us?" Dylan's brow furrowed.

"I have an idea." Stevie stepped toward the table and grabbed Charlie's book. "We'll call them to us. We can use the lighthouse at Cape Lookout." An excited grin tugged on the corners of her mouth. "We'll make it *blink*."

Randy crossed his arms. "Honey, it already blinks."

"Every fifteen seconds to be exact." Ruth scowled.

Stevie tapped the book with her finger. "We can use Morse code."

Dylan stepped forward. "Yes, this is perfect. What message should we send?"

"We have no idea where those witches went," Ruth said. "We can barely see the lighthouse from here. How are they supposed to see it?"

"Not a problem. I can get my media contacts to push the story on the news." Dylan grinned.

Alice's eyes were bright with excitement. "We need something that ties us together, but the rest of the world doesn't know about."

"We have one person in common." A hopeful lightness blossomed in Stevie's chest. "Lucia."

Dylan searched for the Morse code translation on his phone and then set it on the table for all to see. "Dot, dash, dot, dot. Pause. Dot, dot, dash. Pause. Dash, dot, dash, dot. Pause. Dot, dot. Pause. Dot, dash."

"Everyone got it?" Stevie asked.

The coven members nodded.

She opened Charlie's book to the page featuring Cape Lookout. "We'll use this picture to represent the real lighthouse." She reached out to grasp Lexi's and Dylan's hands once more. The other witches closed in and reformed their circle.

Stevie didn't waste a second trying to formulate a rhyming spell. "Just focus on the light. Send the code to it. Remember, we want it to flash at the Cape until someone responds."

They followed her instructions and soon the picture of the lighthouse in the book reflected their combined efforts. Stevie smiled as she watched it flash L-U-C-I-A in a series of dots and dashes. Her simple spell had been successful.

"It is done."

"It is done," her coven echoed. They let go of each other's hands.

Stevie stared through the window. "This storm is showing no signs of letting up. I'll go out to the Cape tomorrow to see if anyone responds to our message."

"I'll go with you." Lexi bounced up on her toes. "We can take a tent in case we have to stay overnight."

"I'll come too." Dylan rested his hand on Stevie's shoulder. Deep lines of worry creased his brow.

Stevie shook her head. "I don't know what to expect from the other group, so I want Charlie to stay home. I'd feel a lot better if you were here with him."

She knew that Dylan wanted to be by her side protecting her from dangers known and unknown. However, with his gift, he was uniquely suited to taking care of Charlie. Her son would be safe with him.

His lips pressed into a thin, fine line. "Okay."

"I'll go with the girls." Deborah cast a wary glance at Dylan. "I'll look after them."

Dylan acknowledged Deborah with a nod. "Thank you." He picked up his phone. "I'll go ahead and call the networks. Wherever the descendants of Lucia's group are, they'll surely hear about this."

Chapter seventeen

Stevie

The next morning, Stevie stood in her living room, assessing the items she'd assembled for her trip to the Cape. Sleeping bags, extra clothes, water, flashlights. Lexi had promised to bring food and a tent. She bit her lip and ran through her mental checklist again. *What have I forgotten?*

Stevie shook her head, frustrated with the anxiety that gnawed at her belly. *It's not like I'm planning a trip across the country.* The Cape wasn't that far away. If they needed something, one of them could always come back and get it.

Deep down, she knew her worries stemmed from something far more dire than a forgotten toothbrush.

Three hundred years had passed since the witches split up, and she had no way of knowing what to expect from another group—assuming anyone answered the call at all. While it was possible that another coven would be happy to connect with more of their kind, it was also possible that they'd all gone as dark as Susan. Their numbers might have swelled to hundreds, or even thousands, over the centuries. Or, the descendants of Lucia's group may have simply died out over time.

There's only one way to find out.

Dylan strode into the living room and, without a word, wrapped his arms around her waist. Stevie inhaled the warm, spicy scent of his cologne and let herself relax in his embrace. While he held her, she sensed all of the worries that he'd left unspoken. She rested her head against his chest and closed her eyes. There was no need to tell him she was worried too. Even with her mental shield in place, she had no doubt he already knew.

Dylan pulled his arms away. "Take my boat, okay? It's fast—"

"In case I need to get away fast. Right?"

"Right." Dylan gave her a quick kiss and paused, just for a moment, to stroke her cheek. "I'll get this stuff loaded up." He nodded toward the pile of supplies.

"Thanks. Lexi and Deborah should be here any minute. I still need to say goodbye to Charlie."

She walked to the staircase and stopped in front of the old portrait of Charlotte, Hannah, and Catherine. Like so many times before, she admired the artist's ability to capture the unique essence of each of Beaufort's first witches—a noble leader, a fierce spirit, and a gentle soul. She wondered what Charlotte would think of her plans to absorb Vanessa's powers and enlist the help of unknown witches.

Stevie shook her head and lowered her gaze, wishing she could just ask her mother for advice instead of trying to commune with a painting. *I miss you, Mom.*

Blinking back the tears that welled in her eyes, she raised her chin. *I'll do whatever it takes to protect our people.* Her attention shifted to the image of Charlotte's oval face. The first queen of the Beaufort witches certainly must have known that feeling. As a descendant of Lucia, the overwhelming need to protect the witches was ingrained in Stevie's biology. It was in her blood, just as it had been in Charlotte's. Just as it had been in her mother's.

"We do what we must," Stevie whispered to the painted figures.

She continued up the stairs and into Charlie's bedroom. She scanned the spacious room, from his neatly made twin bed to the long table in the back on which he displayed his Lincoln Log creations. He wasn't there.

"Charlie." She stepped toward the hidden panel on the interior wall. "I want to talk to you for a minute."

She waited while he swung the wall panel open, revealing the secret room. In the eighteenth century, Charlotte's family had used it to hide people and valuables from raiding pirates and privateers. Now, it served as a quiet space for her little boy.

Stevie forced herself to smile when Charlie poked his head through the open doorway. He showed no intention of leaving his quiet place, so she ducked down and joined him in the small room.

The hidden space gave Charlie a break from light and sound when he needed respite from processing sensory input. Now that his magical gifts had manifested, Stevie suspected that he sometimes sought solace from the effects of his preternatural empathy. Though she'd done her best to protect him from *hearing* about the dangers they faced, there wasn't anything she could do to stop him from *sensing* their feelings about it.

She sat on the floor next to him and watched him trace the edge of his sneaker with his finger. "I think you've noticed that the grownups are unhappy right now."

Charlie nodded, but his focus remained on his shoe.

Wanting to decrease his anxiety without lying, she had to choose her words with care. "I'm going to try to fix our problem. But that means I have to go away for a little while."

Charlie offered no response as he continued to run his finger along his shoe. Stevie listened to his soft breaths for a moment before she continued. "I'm not sure how long I'll be gone. I hope it'll only be a day or two." She knew how much her son hated uncertainties, but it would do no good to lie to him about the timeframe of her trip. "I promise I'll come back home as soon as possible."

Charlie's breaths came faster now, and he began to flick his fingers in front of his eyes. To anyone else, it might have appeared that he was ignoring his mother, but Stevie recognized the signs of his increasing anxiety. Unable to ease his worries, she leaned her head against the wall and closed her eyes. She couldn't tell him when she would come back. She couldn't pacify him with an optimistic platitude. She couldn't even promise that she'd survive through the end of the week.

Stevie opened her eyes and moved to position herself in front of him. She didn't ask him to look at her as he continued to flick his fingers in front his eyes. Her worries were his worries. His pain was her pain. They were united as deeply as any two people could be, but she was the adult. And she knew something he did not.

"It's true that I'm afraid, but we can't give ourselves over to fear. You must remember there's always hope. Do you understand that?"

Charlie's busy hands fell to his lap. His fingers still wiggled, though less frantically than before. Her heart skipped a beat as he granted an all-too-brief glance in her direction. After a moment, he nodded.

She leaned in to ruffle his hair and then gave him a quick kiss on the forehead. "I love you."

Stevie rose to her feet and left the little room, closing the secret panel door behind her. She went back downstairs and poked her head into the living room to find that Dylan had already taken her supplies to the boat.

Deciding to wait on the porch for Lexi and Deborah, Stevie spun around and made her way to the front door. She stepped outside into the cool, dry air and closed the door behind her. The sun hung in the clear blue sky, erasing all traces of the thunderstorm that had raged the night before.

Stevie's phone vibrated in her back pocket. She glanced at its screen and saw that Maura, Charlie's kindergarten teacher, was calling. She groaned, frustrated with herself for forgetting to let her know that he'd be out of school for at least another week. The decision to keep him home again had been difficult since he'd already missed so much class time. But with all of the uncertainty in their immediate future, she believed it was the best thing to do.

She was tempted to decline the call, preferring to postpone mundane school issues until she knew whether or not she would survive her encounter with Susan. She resisted that urge and swiped her finger across the screen to answer the call.

"Hello, Maura." The teacher was a solitary practitioner who'd left a fragrant sachet of herbs in the basket the day after Patricia's funeral. Since she already knew there'd been a death in the family, Stevie skipped over any unnecessary explanations and addressed what she believed was the reason for the call. "I decided to keep Charlie at home a little while longer. I'm sorry I didn't get in touch sooner."

"I have to admit I was worried about Charlie when he didn't come to class today," Maura said. "I'm relieved to hear that he's all right."

"Relieved?" Stevie's brow furrowed. "Did you have a reason to think that he wasn't all right?"

"Well, it's silly, I guess." Maura cleared her throat. "But there are rumors of an unstable woman approaching witches on the boardwalk. Apparently, she claims she has the amulet that sunk with Blackbeard's ship. She also says she's now the new *queen*."

Stevie pursed her lips as Maura's words settled in. The mental image of the dark witch approaching her people as they roamed the waterfront was unsettling enough on its own, but now word had gotten out about the amethyst as well. She'd planned to have the senior coven members relay the information about Susan and the amulet while they worked to recruit witnesses for the Cape Lookout standoff. She'd wanted those revelations to come from *her* camp, not from Susan's.

Stevie let out a resigned sigh. The time had come for truth to reign supreme. *No need to hide anything now.*

"Blackbeard never had the amulet, Maura." Stevie unpacked the whole story for her, beginning with the coven's imprisonment of Susan as well as the reason for it. She explained the true cause of Patricia's death and admitted to the 300-year-long cover up regarding the whereabouts of the magical pendant.

She paused in order to give Maura the opportunity to ask a question if necessary. But the teacher remained silent, no doubt struggling to process the coven's clandestine history.

Stevie raked her hand through her hair before sharing the final piece of news—Susan's demand that they meet at the Cape on Saturday night. "She said that all of you have to come, or she will…kill Charlie."

Maura gasped and whispered the boy's name under her breath.

"She said she won't hurt you; she just wants you all there as witnesses."

"Witnesses to what?"

"She's going to kill me." Stevie gulped. Saying it out loud just made it that much more real.

"No!" Maura's voice pitched higher. "There are hundreds of us. We'll fight her!"

"I'm not asking you to fight. With the amulet, she's stronger than you can possibly imagine. She took on the entire coven without breaking a sweat." Stevie cringed, remembering how Susan had used her vile magic to toss Patricia across the room like a rag doll. "If you fight, she *will* come after you. And I can't guarantee your safety."

"Well, what *can* we do?"

"I could use your help in notifying the others. I need them all to come, for Charlie's sake. Please make sure they understand that they are to be there only as *witnesses*. I don't expect anyone to fight this dark witch on my behalf. Let them know that I want them to protect themselves first." Stevie squeezed her eyes closed. "No matter what happens to me, I want my people to survive."

Chapter eighteen

Vanessa

Vanessa stood in her private bathroom and stared at the floor for several moments, knowing she couldn't avoid the mirror forever. It had been too long since she'd taken a *real* look at her burns. She needed to know if time had begun to heal her wounds. *I have to do this.*

She pressed her lips together and forced herself to raise her head. Staring into her reflection, she focused on her eyes. It was easier to start there. In the wake of all she'd lost, her emerald eyes had remained the same.

She shifted her focus to the red, glazed flesh that marred her complexion. Grotesque ridges and lumps had formed among the burns—permanent reminders of the explosion. Her stomach churned as a wave of nausea rolled through her. The scarring spread all the way across her scalp, where bubbled skin and patches of fuzzy hair crowded the top of her head.

Overcome with disgust, Vanessa slammed her open palm on the mirror, blotting out her face with her disfigured left hand. Hot tears welled in her eyes. First she'd been victimized by her mother and then by Stevie. They had warped her into a pitiable ghost, a shadow of her former self. *Now I live an unending nightmare.*

She turned away from her reflection, pulled up her hood, and stormed into the main living area of the yacht. She didn't want to think anymore. Slumping down on the sofa, she only wanted to tune out—forgetting her scars, the coven, and the ridiculous coup orchestrated by her mother. She clicked on the television using the remote control, technology's weak approximation of magic.

A local weatherman appeared on the screen before a map dotted with numbers and symbols. She couldn't concentrate on any of it. Even his voice smeared into a rumbling background noise, nothing more than a murmur heard through the thick fog of Vanessa's racing mind.

Without warning, the sound from the television cut off, jolting her from her thoughts. As the news program continued in silence on the screen, she raised her head to see Susan coming down from the yacht's deck. *Mother never did tolerate competition well.*

"Good morning." Susan descended the steps into the cabin. "It's a sunny day. Maybe you should spend some time on the deck and get some color on those cheeks." She stopped and brought her hand up to her mouth, issuing a dramatic sigh. "Oh, but your face…maybe it *is* best if you stay down here." She continued her grand entrance. "You can make me some breakfast instead. Preparing for my big day has given me quite an appetite."

Susan had gone away during the night to practice the magic necessary for whatever horrors she planned to inflict on Stevie. Vanessa didn't bother to ask how the practice session went. Her mother's smug grin told her everything she needed to know.

Without a word, Vanessa moved to the galley while Susan selected a fashion magazine from the coffee table and settled in on the sofa. Vanessa grabbed a frying pan from the cupboard and considered voicing a thought that had been on her mind for the last few days. As she gathered the courage to address the topic, she decided to offer her idea as a statement, not a request. If Susan didn't like it, she could always make a better offer.

"Mother, I have made a decision."

Vanessa heard her sharp intake of breath just before Susan plopped the magazine back down on the table. Silence stretched between them for a long moment until her mother twisted around to gape at her.

"A decision?" Susan's thin eyebrows rose. "I wasn't aware that you were in a position to make any decisions. Do go on though. Tell me all about it." Her wide-eyed façade morphed into a steely glare as she awaited an explanation.

Vanessa hesitated, certain now that nothing good would come from stating her plan. However, she had no choice but to finish what she had started. "I want to…I mean…I *am* going to see a plastic surgeon." She waited for an automatic rebuke that did not come. "Will you stop me?"

Susan's mouth drew up in a slow smile as she rose from the couch and stepped toward the counter separating the galley from the living area. With her head tilted and her brows raised, she projected a near perfect illusion of bewilderment. But Vanessa saw an unmistakable cunning confidence lurking in her mother's eyes.

"Why, there's no need to go to that trouble." Susan waved her hand. "After Saturday's…festivities, I will make you beautiful once again! All you have to do is stand with me and show your loyalty while I deal with Stevie. Support me in front of the witnesses, and I will reward you by fixing your face. I'll order that old doctor to heal you. He can do a better job of it than a plastic surgeon could anyway." She scowled as she gestured toward the top of Vanessa's head. "I'll even have him give you some hair."

Though she knew the magical healing depended on whether or not she managed to keep her mother happy, this was the first time Susan had been specific about a timeline, as well as her expectations.

Now Vanessa had hope. "I'd like that, Mother." She cracked an egg and dropped its contents into the hot frying pan. "But, why wait? Why not heal me now?"

"Just think of how this will look to my subjects." Susan gestured to her scars. "We have, in you, a visual representation of the coven's cruelty and destructive nature. We'll show them how Patricia's spawn and her hateful inner circle damaged you and turned you into a...*hideous* monster. Then, when my enemies are dead and their followers are kneeling at my feet, I'll restore you to your former beauty."

"Will you restore my powers as well?"

Susan stepped away from the counter and gazed through the window, staring at nothing in particular. "Possibly."

Her mother's vague response came as no surprise. Susan needed something to lord over her. She would never commit to relinquishing all of her control at once.

But the amulet wasn't the only way to restore her powers. *If I could just get my hands on the safe...*

Susan continued to weave her prophecy. "Think of it. I'll expose the coven's darkness and heal your wounds, with all of my subjects standing in witness. The witches of Beaufort will know, without a doubt, that I'm a mighty queen, *and* I'm generous to those who serve me well. Yes, I think this will work nicely." She nodded slowly in apparent appreciation of her own brilliance.

Susan had a certain gleam in her eye now. Vanessa suspected that the vision of impending triumph played out in her mother's mind, flush with fresh new details. Perhaps she had tweaked the imagined outcome, visualizing an even more glorious victory.

Vanessa loaded the egg onto a plate and carried it to her mother.

Susan didn't bother to look at the food before she pushed it away. "I'm not hungry anymore."

Vanessa clenched her teeth and trudged back to the galley with the untouched breakfast. Accommodating her mother was not unlike caring for a disagreeable toddler.

With her nose high in the air, Susan strolled back toward the sofa and sat down. "It won't be long now. Soon Stevie and the boy will be gone, and then everyone will know *I* am the true queen."

Vanessa bit her lip at the mention of Charlie. "Why kill the kid? He's no threat to you."

Bitter darkness shadowed Susan's features. "He's the last of Lucia's line—he has to die! If I let him grow up, he might sire a daughter. If that happens, she could try to lay claim to my amulet."

Vanessa's shoulders drew up as she stepped closer to the sofa. "But that would be years away, if it even happens at all. What's the rush?"

"When did you get so soft? It sounds like you actually care about that kid." Susan narrowed her eyes and wagged her finger at Vanessa. "Stop arguing with me about it. You have no say in this."

Vanessa couldn't deny her fondness for the boy. She might not have any love for Stevie or the coven, but the boy was different. *There's something special about him.*

"I just think—"

"Look at that!" Susan hunched forward, staring at the television. She waved her hand and the sound of the news broadcast filled the cabin once again.

On the screen, a young blond reporter stood in front of the Cape Lookout Lighthouse. "No one knows why the lighthouse began blinking this strange pattern or how to stop it." The camera panned to a shot of park officials hurrying into the tower. An inset image of the lighthouse at night filled the corner of the screen, its light flashed bold against the black sky. "Sources tell us that it's sending some sort of message in Morse code." The reporter translated the blinking dots and dashes, "L-U-C-I-A."

Susan sank back as the reporter continued her coverage of the strange story. "Well, now. *This* is an interesting development."

Chapter nineteen

Stevie

Stevie stood on Dylan's dock alongside Deborah and Lexi. She eyed the sleek, new speedboat with unease. It was just like the one she'd destroyed—with Vanessa on it. Cringing at the memory, she figured that there were bits and pieces of that vessel still washing ashore on various nearby beaches.

Lexi passed a small cooler to Dylan, who stood on board. Stevie couldn't recall the last time she'd seen her best friend wear jeans and sweatshirt. Even dressed in casual attire, Lexi managed to appear runway ready.

Dylan grabbed Deborah's canvas tote bag, which held her knitting supplies, and tucked it in place beside the cooler. Clearly, the older witch planned to continue working her own unique brand of magic while they were away. *Good. I'll take all the help I can get right now.*

"It's hard to believe that we might finally be reunited with the rest our people." Deborah's broad grin telegraphed her excitement. "I think your mother would be very proud of you for thinking of this."

Her joy, though not quite infectious, had an impact on Stevie. A twinge of optimism gnawed at the edges of her anxiety.

Lexi hopped aboard the boat as Dylan stepped out and onto the dock. When he glanced at Stevie, she spotted the deep lines of worry etched on his forehead. She knew right away that he remained immune to Deborah's excitement.

"The key is in the ignition." He gestured toward the console. "Are you ready?"

She gave a slight nod. "As ready as I can be."

He hugged her and held her close for a long moment. "Be careful."

Stevie rested her head against his chest, wishing she could stay in his embrace forever. "I will." She pulled away with reluctance.

Lexi extended her hand toward Deborah, who'd remained on the dock. "Come on, Mom. I'll help you get in."

Deborah gripped the side of her wide-brimmed hat, her long graying hair flitted in the breeze. "You don't have to treat me like a little old lady, you know. I was jumping into boats long before you were just a sweet backrub from your father."

"Ew, Mom!"

Deborah chuckled as she accepted Lexi's extended hand. "Well, it was a *very* nice backrub." She stepped onto the boat and settled into one of the vinyl bench seats.

Grinning at their exchange, Stevie glanced at Dylan. "I guess it's time to go. I'll check in with you later." She made her way onboard.

Dylan freed the vessel from its ties to the dock as Stevie started the engine. She guided the boat away from home and toward an uncertain future. Idling as she crossed the No Wake

119

Zone of Taylor's Creek, she maneuvered into the channel that would take them to Cape Lookout—where they would find a certain magically misbehaving lighthouse.

Stevie cranked the throttle forward. The boat rose up slightly as it stopped its slow plow through the water and started to skim across its surface. She caught sight of the lighthouse in the distance and adjusted the boat's angle to head for it, keeping an eye out for lighter, choppier water that would indicate sand bars and shallows below.

The wind blew Stevie's hair away from her face as the salty spray dotted her skin. In spite of her anxiety, the sense of freedom that came with being on the open water buoyed her heart. She stole a quick glance at Lexi and Deborah. Seeing both of their smiles, she knew they felt the same way.

They cruised past the nine mile long stretch of barrier island known as Shackleford Banks. She glimpsed a small herd of wild horses nibbling on the marsh grasses while a few others roamed free along the shore of the uninhabited island. Ahead of her, a brown pelican swooped down, scooping an unsuspecting fish from the water.

The lighthouse grew taller as she steered the boat toward Cape Lookout. Its vivid black and white diamond pattern stood in stark contrast against the clear blue sky beyond it. Stevie had captured the same stunning image in numerous photographs, which had always been best sellers in her shop.

Taking in the sight of the two-story house that stood near the tower, she recalled Sam's spiel about the history of the old building. On one of their earliest dates, he'd shared with her that it had once served as the residence for the lighthouse keepers and their families. Before electricity, the care and maintenance of the light had been much more involved, requiring the attention of three on-site attendants. Among countless other tasks, the keepers also had the grueling chore of hauling heavy cans of oil up the 216 steps to the lantern room every day. Now, the Coast Guard handled the important work of maintaining the light. She smiled, remembering Sam's enthusiasm for the Cape's history. *I bet he tells all his water taxi customers about the Keeper's Quarters—whether they want to hear it or not.*

Stevie anchored the speedboat just offshore, and they began to unload their supplies. There were few visitors roaming the island's beach, which wasn't surprising for a weekday in the fall. By the time the passenger ferries stopped running and the visitors' center closed in the afternoon, they might even have the island to themselves. She hoped the same would hold true for Saturday night. Whatever Susan had planned, Stevie didn't want any non-witches to witness it.

A bustle of activity surrounded the lighthouse itself. A female reporter stood near the base of the tower and spoke into a handheld microphone while a single cameraman filmed her. As the light continued to blink its Morse code signal, a couple of park rangers in olive drab uniforms conversed with tool belt wearing workers. One gestured toward the flashing light atop the tower, and then he shrugged his shoulders. A coast guard officer emerged from the building, appearing just as baffled as the others did.

"Is there anything they can do to stop the signal?" Stevie asked.

Deborah shook her head. "I suppose they could turn off the light altogether, but I doubt they'd do that. It would be too dangerous for passing ships."

Stevie, Lexi, and Deborah carried their gear further south down the island. They chose a spot on the sound side of the beach that was well away from the ferry dock but still within clear view of the lighthouse and the keeper's quarters. If anyone came looking for them, they would be easy enough to find.

Stevie set up the beach chairs in a semi-circle near the dunes, with the center chair facing the sound. The placement of the other two chairs would allow the witches to see if anyone approached from either direction along the shore. They all worked together to construct the small tent that they would share during the night. Once they had settled their campsite, they eased into their chairs and began the indefinite wait for the possible arrival of other witches. Deborah set to work on her knitting right away, once again selecting protective white yarn for her magical work.

Maybe she's aware of the dangers involved in reaching out to the descendants of Lucia's group after all.

Stevie leaned in close to Lexi. "I want you to take Charlie and leave on Friday. I don't want him to see…" She paused, unable to finish the sentence. "Please just take him far away from here and don't bring him back until you know it's safe."

Lexi's eyes grew wide. "I'll do whatever you need, but doesn't Sam usually take Charlie on the weekends?"

"Yes, but he'll be safer with one of us." Stevie stared out over the water. "I'll take care of Sam." Somehow, she'd have to come up with a reasonable excuse for Charlie to miss yet another weekend visitation with his father. She hated lying to him, but she knew of no other way.

They sat in companionable silence as the day wore on. Deborah continued knitting while Stevie and Lexi assessed the few people who wandered along the beach. Stevie tensed as a boat neared the shore and then sailed off toward the open ocean. So far, no new witches had appeared.

"How long do you think we should wait?" Lexi asked.

Stevie shrugged. "I'm willing to give it a couple of days. If they're still out there somewhere, we don't know how far they would have to travel to get here."

"What if no one comes?"

"We'll cross that bridge when we come to it." Deborah glanced up from her knitting. "Don't give up hope yet."

Stevie's stomach let out a gurgling rumble. "I'm starving. What did you bring to eat?"

"Granola bars." Lexi stood up and began to rummage through her backpack. "Ah, here you go." She passed one to Stevie and another to Deborah.

Stevie pursed her lips in disappointment as she removed the wrapper from the small bar. She wished they had brought Alice along on the trip. She could easily change this granola bar into the pizza Stevie really wanted.

Of all the times for my appetite to come back.

Hours passed and, by late afternoon, all of the shell collectors and beach walkers had left the island. They hadn't seen any other people in a long while. In the quiet that Stevie would have once found serene, her tenuous optimism began to fade. Once again, her thoughts drifted to her upcoming encounter with Susan.

She leaned toward Deborah. "Will Charlie become king when I die?"

Deborah stopped knitting and raised her head to meet Stevie's gaze. "We've never had a king. There has *always* been a girl child to succeed the queen."

"Well, I'm not going to have any more children." She had been so certain of her decision, she'd insisted that Sam have a vasectomy years earlier, right after Charlie received his autism diagnosis. At the time, she'd been so overwhelmed with the information and the bleak prognosis of her son's condition, she was sure she couldn't handle the additional responsibility of having another child. Charlie's symptoms had improved since that time, far beyond the early predictions of his specialists. But was it enough to make her reconsider her position? She couldn't say.

She hadn't discussed the possibility of children with Dylan. In fact, they hadn't talked about their future at all. She gulped. *It doesn't matter now anyway. My days are numbered.*

"Then who will lead the coven when Susan kills me?"

Deborah had resumed her knitting. "We'll cross that bridge when we come to it...*if* we come to it."

Frustrated, Stevie rose from her chair and began to wander up the beach toward the lighthouse. The rangers and workers had all left the island, unsuccessful in sorting out the mystery of the secret code. *They'll probably be back at it again tomorrow.*

When Stevie reached the beacon, she stood at the base of the one hundred and sixty-three foot tall tower and looked up, something she had done many times throughout her childhood. From this angle, the lighthouse seemed to tilt forward, causing the familiar thrill of vertigo to wash over her. For a moment, she believed the entire structure might topple, crashing down upon her with the weight of its long history as the guardian of the shore.

It occurred to Stevie that she could cut down the mighty tower with little more than a thought. With a bit of cleverly dispensed magic, she could shift the sand on which it stood and destroy the landmark forever.

What would protect boaters from the treacherous North Carolina coastline then?

Nothing. Without a guardian, their existence would continue only at the mercy of the sea.

And the sea could be a volatile bitch.

Chapter twenty

Stevie

The temperature dropped when the sun went down on Monday night. Stevie shivered and pulled her fleece blanket tighter against her shoulders.

Lexi wrapped her arms around herself. "Let's get a fire going."

"Good idea." Deborah nodded. "My hands are almost too cold for knitting."

"We'll have to find some wood to burn." Stevie scanned their immediate area. "I wish we'd thought of this earlier when we had more light. It's going to be hard to find any now."

Deborah chuckled. "I sometimes forget that all of this is still very new to you, Stevie." She passed one of her knitting needles to Lexi. "Here you go, dear."

"Perfect. Thanks, Mom." Lexi knelt down in front of her chair. She pressed the tip of the long, metal needle into the soft sand and began to guide it with her hand. First, she carved a circle. Then, within the confines of that shape, she drew a short stack of what appeared to be wooden sticks.

Stevie tilted her head as she watched her friend work. Lexi exuded the same calm confidence she possessed when she worked on one of her paintings.

Lexi continued to her task, drawing wispy shapes that extended out from the drawing of crisscrossed wood in the center of her circle. *Flames.*

Satisfied with her work, Lexi stood up and handed the knitting needle back to Deborah. She glanced quickly up and down the beach, confirming that they were still alone. Then she held her delicate hands over her artwork in the sand.

The witches remained silent as Lexi focused her energy. Almost instantly, her drawing became three-dimensional. The drawn wood rose up from the sand, at first translucent and then darkening to a grayish brown. A tiny, red flame bloomed within the pile of kindling. It began to grow, creeping beneath the wood until orange flames licked the air.

"That's nice, dear." Deborah warmed her hands over the fire. "Thank you."

Another hour had passed with no sign of anyone responding to their signal. Certain that no one would come out to the island at this late hour, Stevie focused on a new task—a good-bye letter to Charlie. If she didn't survive her encounter with Susan, she wanted to leave something behind for him, just as Patricia had done for her.

Lexi's magical fire and the battery-powered lantern by her side provided just enough light for her to see the blank page before her. How could she begin to tell her son how much she loved him? The few words that came to her mind were wholly insufficient to express all that she wanted him to know. Trying to ignore the hollow ache in her chest, she wondered if her mother had endured the same agony when she forged her final letter.

Stevie chewed on the top of her pen and watched the surface of the sound. Moonlight danced on the tips of the choppy waves as they made their way to the shore. Beneath those glimmers of silver light, black water hid both the beauties and the dangers that lurked below. She raised her head toward the low hung moon. Now a waxing gibbous, it grew fatter with each passing evening, like the headlamp of an oncoming train. Soon, it would be completely full, and when that night came, she would stand before Susan. Inadequate but determined. Helpless but hopeful.

Seeking a distraction from her morbid thoughts, she stole a glimpse of her companions. Deborah continued the quiet work of her protection spell, and Stevie wondered if her hands ever grew tired from their constant motion. Lexi busied herself studying the pictures in the latest gossip magazine. Satisfied to read only the captions under the pictures, she didn't delve into the substance of the full articles.

If there were any other campers on the island, Stevie had neither seen nor heard them. Unable to focus on the letter she wished she didn't have to write, her attention wandered back to the waters just offshore. She listened to the steady thrum of waves washing onto the beach. Narrowing her eyes, she examined the view that she'd been watching all evening.

Something's different.

The lighthouse continued to flash its secret message while Stevie stared out over the water. She furrowed her brow as she glanced up and down the beach. No one was there, and yet, she didn't feel as though they were alone. She sat up straighter in her chair and then slipped her notepad and pen into her backpack.

"Stevie?" Lexi leaned forward, "What's wrong?"

"Nothing, I guess. It's just that I…"

"I feel it too." Deborah returned her knitting to her canvas tote. "Someone's here."

"Where?" Lexi twisted in her seat to look behind her. "I don't see anyone."

"Neither do I," Stevie said.

"That doesn't necessarily mean we're alone." A hint of a smile curled the corners of Deborah's lips. Whatever she sensed, it wasn't danger.

Stevie remained alert; her eyes darted from one direction on the beach to the next. The island came to life as her awareness grew even more heightened. Each movement commanded her attention—a crab scurrying along the water's edge, seagrass rustling in the wind, a cloud floating in front of the moon. Sound and motion surrounded them, but none of it signaled the presence of other people. Lexi stood and examined the dunes behind them, to no avail. Deborah crossed her arms and leaned back in her chair, though she too kept a faithful watch.

Finally, Stevie had enough of watching and waiting. They weren't alone. She knew it. What she didn't know was who waited in the shadows. Was it a friend or an enemy?

"Enough!" Stevie shouted as she jumped up from her chair. "We know you're here!"

Lexi rushed to Stevie's side. "Stop hiding!"

Deborah rose to her feet as well. "There." She nodded toward the southern end of the beach.

Stevie narrowed her eyes, focusing on the two figures now moving toward them, a man and a woman. Tall and willowy, the woman had straight black hair that blew freely in the wind. The man had a sturdier build. As they drew closer, Stevie could see that he also had long hair, though he had pulled his back in a ponytail. They both appeared to be several years older than Stevie and Lexi.

"Just look at those biceps," Lexi whispered. "Do you think they're a couple? Maybe they're brother and sister." She crossed her fingers. "Please let them be siblings."

"Seriously?" Stevie scowled at Lexi. "That's what you're thinking about right now?"

Deborah grinned. "I bet he could give a *really* good back rub."

"Okay, you're not helping." Stevie propped a hand on her hip.

Lexi kept her voice low. "They're part of the other group, Stevie. They're witches for sure. I can see it in their auras."

Deborah's grin broadened. "They answered our call."

Goose bumps rose up on Stevie's arms. They had connected with Lucia's group. What that meant for the future of her people, she still didn't know. But she understood that she'd crossed a 300-year-old line.

There's no going back now.

When the man and woman drew close to their campsite, Stevie stepped forward to greet them, with Lexi and Deborah at her side. She could see more details of their features now. Both shared the same dark complexion, deep-set eyes, and straight noses. Stevie suspected that they were not only siblings, but it was possible they were twins. Lexi would surely be pleased with that turn of events.

"Hello." Stevie tried not to grimace at her own awkwardness, but she could think of no other way to greet the others.

The woman met Stevie's gaze with cold, dark eyes and then jutted her chin toward the flashing light emitting from the lighthouse. "Did you do that?"

Stevie nodded. "We did."

There was no glimmer of kindness in the woman's expression. "Then we have something to discuss, don't we?"

"Yes, I suppose we do." Stevie gave a curt nod. She gestured toward the semi-circle of beach chairs. "Please, have a seat."

"No, thank you." The woman's shoulders remained rigid. "I prefer to stand."

Lexi cleared her throat and bounced forward. "I think introductions are in order. I'm Lexi." She pointed toward her mother. "And this is my mom, Deborah."

Deborah offered a cordial smile to the stone-faced woman and then tilted her head toward Stevie. "This is Stevie, our queen."

No one's ever introduced me as the queen before. It seemed so formal and antiquated. A rush of heat rose in Stevie's cheeks. Though she still wasn't comfortable with the title, she could not help but notice that the woman didn't kneel in acknowledgement of her status.

"I'm Kara," the dark-haired woman said. "And this is my brother, Kyle."

Without a trace of his sister's apprehensive animosity, he smiled. "Nice to meet you." He spoke with a surprising gentleness—nothing at all like the caveman style grunts she'd expected to hear from the muscle-bound man.

"Nice to meet you too." Stevie extended her hand to welcome the witches.

Kara eyed Stevie's outstretched arm with suspicion before she acquiesced and gave her a half-hearted handshake. "I'm the leader of the Wilmington witches."

Stevie now understood her cold greeting. As her counterpart, Kara had to act in the best interest of her own people. *She probably has the same laundry list of misgivings about connecting with another group of witches that I have.* Studying Kara's frosty expression, Stevie guessed that the other woman had come to the Cape not out of a sense of community but to investigate—and perhaps even eliminate—a threat.

"Wilmington?" Lexi asked. "That's not far from here at all."

Deborah arched her eyebrow. "How have we gone this long without bumping into each other?"

"We've known about your group since Blackbeard took Charlotte, Hannah, and Catherine," Kara explained without emotion. "However, Lucia left us with strict instructions to stay away from you. Our groups were to remain separate to ensure our mutual survival."

"Then why did you come?" Stevie asked.

Kara glanced toward the blinking beacon atop the lighthouse once again. "Lucia's final words were, 'Heed the call of the Diamond Lady.' Today, she called." Kara eyed Stevie narrowly. "Now, why are *you* here?"

Stevie inhaled a deep breath of salty ocean air before launching into her tale of Susan's vile history. She told Kara all about Susan's murderous ways and of the coven's attempt to keep her imprisoned in a psychiatric hospital. To cap it off, she explained how Patricia lost the amulet and ultimately met her demise at the hands of the dark witch.

Kara's stony gaze gave way to a scowl when she heard the news of the stolen amulet. "Even in Wilmington, we know the sacred duty of protecting the amethyst. I don't understand how Patricia managed to lose it." She shook her head. "What a shame."

Stevie clenched her jaw. "My people, *my family*, have kept the amulet safe through countless generations. This time, we simply had a perfect storm of events. For starters, my mother was very sick…"

Lexi stepped forward. "Patricia was a good queen. You have no right to judge her."

Kyle placed his hand on Lexi's arm. "I'm sure Patricia was a fine queen. My sister didn't mean to offend you." His soothing voice pacified Lexi right away.

Kara remained silent. Stevie found it impossible to read her expression. As far as she was concerned, whether the leader had intended offense remained in question.

Stevie continued to explain their dire situation. She made sure Kara understood that Susan now possessed almost omnipotent power between her own extraordinary gifts and the magic provided by the amulet. She explained that Susan intended to rule over all of the witches and would certainly seek to destroy Stevie when they met on Saturday night.

Kara's brow furrowed. "It sounds like she's willing to kill anyone who stands in her way. With that kind of power, I'm not sure she can be stopped." She looked down at the sand. "I can't send my people into a blood bath."

"I know." Stevie gulped back her disappointment. Some part of her had hoped the other group would know how to defeat the dark witch. Now, after meeting Kara and Kyle, she knew she didn't want to risk harm to the Wilmington witches any more than she wanted her own people in the line of fire. "Believe me, I know. But I'm not asking you to bring them to fight. I only want them there as witnesses."

"You think their presence will deter Susan? It won't work." Kara scoffed and shook her head. "Besides, as soon as she realizes who we are, she'll come after my group. I can't risk that."

"We may live apart, but Stevie is still your queen. Remember that." Deborah punctuated her statement with a sharp nod.

Kara bristled. "I have a responsibility to protect my own people. I am their leader." She pursed her lips and tilted her head as though she were deep in thought. Kyle assumed a similar stance and shared an intense glance with his sister.

Telepathy. Stevie's stomach clenched as she awaited the outcome of their wordless discussion.

After a moment, Kara nodded in unspoken acknowledgement. "I'll tell my people about your plight. However, I will not order them to come to your assistance. They're free to choose their own path."

Stevie heaved a sigh and nodded. "That's all I can ask. Thank you." They exchanged contact information and made plans to meet again later in the week.

In spite of their lengthy discussion, Stevie realized that she knew very little about the Wilmington witches.

"How many are in your group?" Stevie asked.

"We have plenty." Kara waved her arm, and a powerboat appeared just offshore.

Lexi gasped and pointed to the vessel. "How long has that been there?"

"Since before sunset." Kyle said. "We had to make sure it was safe to meet with you. We've been in hiding a long time."

"Yeah, I get that." Lexi couldn't take her eyes off the boat, which had been anchored less than thirty yards in front of them for hours. "But how…how did you do that?"

Kyle grinned. "It's a skill that has been passed down among our people since the eighteenth century. We could hide this entire island if we had to."

Chapter twenty-one

Stevie

Stevie arrived home early the next morning. Even under the magical protections of a salt circle, a fervently knitted blanket, and gemstones, she felt anything but safe. She sat at her kitchen table, trying to form a functional strategy to combat Susan. She wanted to offer some semblance of hope when she met with her coven on Wednesday.

Once again, she considered her plan to absorb Vanessa's bound powers—something she couldn't share with the others. It remained their best chance of defeating Susan. She bit her lip, listening to the whimsical music coming from the television in the den. With Dylan and Charlie just down the hall, she couldn't go through it with it now. *Soon though. Soon.*

She slumped against the back of the chair. Exhaustion and stress weaved together in her mind to form a tapestry of dire scenarios for herself, her loved ones, and all of the witches she had a duty to protect. Her lighthouse gambit had paid some dividends, but the involvement of the Wilmington witches remained uncertain. Even if they chose to help, tremendous risk remained. Again and again, her thoughts wandered back to a tangled loop of unanswered questions.

She knew there would be a cost to any victory, great or small, against the combined might of Susan and the amulet. What right did she have to enmesh another group of witches in her problems? They owed her nothing. They certainly did not owe her the lives that would be at risk if they joined her half-formed plan. Did their presence provide any real advantage over the unstoppable power Susan possessed? Would it make any difference at all?

Stevie shook her head as if to pull free from the unending cycle of questions without answers. She immediately regretted the sudden movement. Anxiety had twisted her shoulders into a knot of intense pain, and now her head throbbed as well.

Her own mortality weighed on her mind. The witches of Beaufort had no idea of the darkness that would rain down on them in the event of her death. Eliminating Stevie could not possibly be enough to satisfy Susan. She would always crave more power, more control, more blood. Her need to penalize the coven for her incarceration, along with her innate cruelty, would bring suffering unlike anything they had seen before. The old terror of witch hunts would pale in comparison.

As big as those worries were, her thoughts circled closer to home. How would her father handle her death so soon after the loss of his wife? What would happen to Charlie?

Stevie closed her eyes and rubbed her temples, trying to ease the thunderous ache in her head. She had a closet full of herbal remedies gifted to her by her loyal followers, but she couldn't recall which plant was best for curing any particular ailment. *Basic witch knowledge. How am I supposed to lead these people when I can't even cure a simple headache?*

Charlie appeared in the doorway, his face impassive. He stepped toward the table and hauled himself into a chair. Dylan followed him, holding the little boy's tablet and grinning.

As usual, Stevie would have to guess what Charlie wanted. Since he'd come to the kitchen, her options narrowed a bit. "Are you—?"

Dylan cut her off with a loud cough. She looked up at him and tilted her head, confused. He placed a finger over his lips, urging her to remain quiet.

Stevie turned her attention to Charlie, who sat with her at the table, his gaze remained focused on his folded hands. After a long moment, he raised his head and glanced in her direction.

He opened his mouth to speak. "Are you thirsty, Charlie?"

The world stood still. Nothing else existed in that moment except for Charlie. Stevie's headache faded away and her hands began to tremble. Her son had just spoken a complete sentence. Imperfect perhaps, but complete nonetheless.

Dylan leaned forward, eyes wide with excitement. "He means—"

"I know exactly what he means." Stevie drew her shaky hand to her mouth.

Charlie had repeated the sentence that he'd always heard just before Stevie gave him a drink. *He'd known what he wanted, and he'd asked for it.*

Stevie struggled to keep her emotions in check. An overly enthusiastic response might startle him, and tears would confuse him.

Are you thirsty, Charlie? The words rang in her mind like sleigh bells on Christmas. She considered correcting him but decided against it. Not now. Not in such a monumental moment. More words would come. There would be opportunities to practice syntax and context later. In time, she'd teach him that he didn't have to ask himself for a drink.

"Okay, I'll get you some water." Stevie's voice quaked with emotion. She rose from the table and made her way to the cupboard. She glanced back at Dylan, who had been watching her with tears in his eyes. Her heart pounded with joy as she selected a cup, filled it with water, and carried it back to Charlie. After placing it on the table, she kissed the top of his head. "Good job."

Stevie leaned in close to Dylan. "Did you know he was going to do this?"

He turned Charlie's tablet over and showed Stevie the screen. Her son had typed *Are you thirsty, Charlie?* over and over again. "He's been practicing it in his head for a while."

Stevie rested her hand on her chest. She couldn't wait to see what Charlie accomplished next…assuming she lived long enough to witness it.

Chapter twenty-two

Vanessa

Vanessa sat at the deck table on Wednesday night. Thick cloud cover had hidden the moon and stars from view, blanketing her in the darkness she preferred. The dim glow from nearby streetlamps and businesses supplied just enough illumination to see, but not enough to expose. She sighed and drank in the comfort of this quiet solitude, peace in invisibility.

A cold, salty breeze blew in across the black waters of Taylor's Creek. She took it head on, allowing it to wash over her. Her hood flapped and then fell back onto her shoulders, revealing the scars on her face and scalp. She gasped and hurried to pull the cover back over her head. Even alone in the darkness, she wasn't willing to lay those wounds bare.

Only a few more days to go.

The cabin door swung open, and Susan emerged onto the deck—unusually sober given the late hour. She strolled over to the chaise and settled in with a satisfied sigh. Plucking the binoculars from the side table, she began her obsessive ritual of watching Stevie's house.

Vanessa studied her mother for a moment. She knew very little about the woman who had raised her. Had she always been like this? Vanessa couldn't say for sure. Memories of her early childhood were murky at best, but she could not recall a time when Susan had been satisfied with her circumstances. She could only remember a deep and abiding need to please her mother at any cost.

Some things never change.

She straightened the cuff of her sweatshirt and wondered how she'd spend her time once the business with the coven was over. Since she'd left the hospital, her days began and ended on the yacht, her floating prison. If Susan healed her scars, she could go back to Los Angeles and resume her former career. Breaking narcissistic millionaires with their own infidelity had proven to be a lucrative business for her. And, it was something she could do without her magic.

Imagining a future without her powers restored left her with a knot in her stomach, and knowing that her magic was somewhere inside Stevie's house was almost too much to bear. She wanted nothing more than to walk right into that house and take back what the coven had stolen from her.

No opportunity to recover the safe had presented itself since she had watched Stevie carry it across the street. She would need near perfect conditions just to get to it. For starters, her mother would have to be otherwise and thoroughly engaged. Given her penchant for spying on Stevie with those binoculars, Vanessa's odds of approaching the house without detection were limited. In addition, Stevie's home had been a hub of activity all week. According to Susan's play-by-play reports, the coven members were coming and going at regular intervals, and Dylan appeared to have moved in with her. That place was never empty, and Stevie was never alone.

It had been enough of a challenge just to leave the candle on the porch. To actually go inside was another matter altogether. She blinked, remembering the moment of weakness that had inspired her to align herself with the coven. It had been a stupid move. Risky and desperate. *I'm better off with my mother.*

She still didn't know what Stevie's intentions were with the safe. If she meant to absorb her magic, had she already done so? If not, then perhaps her powers would still be available after Susan eliminated Stevie. By then, her house would be empty too.

Vanessa couldn't bring herself to cling to the hope that her mother would restore her powers. Nor did she want to wait for Stevie to die before she retrieved the safe. Her magic could be long gone by then—if it wasn't already.

"Hmm. It looks like the faux queen is holding another coven meeting." Susan held the binoculars to her eyes as she leaned back in the chaise. "The old ones arrived a few minutes ago. The little slutty one and her mother are walking toward the house now. Do you think they're going to devise a strategy to defeat me?" She threw her head back and laughed.

Surely, Stevie knew that Susan would kill her, but did she know that Charlie's fate was sealed as well?

Susan's sneer faded when she peered through the lenses once more. "I haven't seen that car before or the two people who just stepped out of it." She held the binoculars out for Vanessa. "Here. See if you recognize them."

Vanessa stepped across the deck to her mother's side to accept the magically enhanced field glasses. She drew them up and stared down the length of Front Street in the direction of Stevie's house. She viewed the unfamiliar Jeep parked by the curb and the dark haired couple who had emerged from it. "I don't know them." She shrugged and handed the binoculars back to her mother.

"I wonder if they were successful with their lighthouse trick." Susan glanced at Vanessa. "Maybe those two are descendants of Lucia's group. Wouldn't it be something to have our scattered tribes reunited? I guess Stevie wants to make sure there are plenty of witnesses to her death."

"If she has gathered more witches, I would think that means she intends to fight." Vanessa pursed her lips.

"Well, I can't imagine that she called them here to welcome me as their queen." Susan snickered. "This is a good thing. Saves me the trouble of tracking them down."

"We don't know how many are in the other group." Vanessa stared in the direction of Stevie's house, though buildings and trees obstructed her view. "How can you be so sure you'll win a fight against *all* of them?"

Susan clutched the enormous amethyst pendant. "Queens of ancient times said this amulet possessed the power of a thousand witches."

"Still, if that's a whole new group, we don't know how many witches there are now. If they all turn on you—"

"Don't be ridiculous!" Susan snapped her head toward Vanessa. "The witches of ancient times were pure-blooded, far superior to anyone in our time. Our blood grows more diluted with each generation. Without the help of the amulet, modern witches are barely stronger than newborn kittens. It doesn't matter how many soldiers she adds to her idiot army. They can't stop me."

Vanessa's mouth went dry. *This standoff will be a massacre.*

"By reuniting our people, Stevie has only succeeded in growing my kingdom. They'll all kneel before me, or they will die."

Susan placed the binoculars on the table and then rose from the chaise. "I'm going out to the Cape to practice my surprise. I want everything to go perfectly, especially in front of all those uninvited guests."

Vanessa shuddered as Susan disappeared before her eyes. Her mother had begun practicing the darkest, most dangerous magic by opening the veil and consorting with demons. Vanessa wanted no part of it.

But she had no choice.

chapter twenty-three

Stevie

As the coven members settled in the living room, Stevie cast a wary glance at the two chairs that remained empty. Kara had given no commitment to attend the meeting, leaving Stevie with little confidence she would receive any support from the Wilmington group.

But Alice, Deborah, Ruth, Randy, Lexi and Dylan all stood ready to help. Though she was grateful for their willingness to take on Susan, she couldn't deny the guilt that weighed on her shoulders. She loved them all. If they tried to defend her against the dark witch, they would perish as well. Regardless of her fate, she wanted her people to survive.

The slam of a car door jarred her from her worries.

"They're here!" Lexi jumped up from her chair and hurried toward the front door. "I'll let them in."

Stevie heard the heavy door swing open before Kara and Kyle had a chance to knock. She listened as Lexi greeted them and offered to take their jackets.

"No thank you." Kara's icy tone echoed into the living room. "We'll keep them. We won't stay long."

Stevie's heart sank. Kara sounded just as indifferent as she had when they'd met on Cape Lookout.

Lexi led the two guests into the living room and introduced them to Dylan, Ruth, Randy, and Alice.

Deborah smiled. "It's good to see you again."

"Thanks for coming tonight." Stevie forced herself to smile when she greeted them.

Without a word, Kara nodded and settled into one of the empty chairs. Her brother followed suit.

Stevie cleared her throat and addressed Kara. "Alice, Ruth, and Randy have been working on contacting the solitary witches of Beaufort. They've explained that I don't expect anyone to risk their life in a fight against Susan. However, if they *choose* to defend me, I will welcome their help. I believe they can support our efforts without drawing too much attention to themselves and therefore remain out of Susan's crosshairs. We'll discuss that more in a bit."

"How many do you have?" Kara asked.

Alice leaned forward. "Our numbers have dwindled in recent generations, so we don't have as many to call on as we might have once had. As of the last count, we have about two hundred who have promised to come. I suspect there will be even more as we get closer to Saturday. The only ones who refused were some of the older witches who felt they were too frail to make the trip to the Cape. Of course, we didn't contact any of the children or teenagers."

Stevie nodded to Alice and then shifted her attention back to Kara. "What about you? How many will come from Wilmington?"

"The number isn't important." Kara spoke to the entire coven but avoided making eye contact with Stevie. "This dark witch is a serious threat as long as she has the amulet. The combined power of both of our groups wouldn't be enough to stop her."

Dylan's hands curled into fists. "We won't stand by and watch Susan kill Stevie. We have to *do* something!"

Kara's dispassionate gaze shifted to Dylan. "I can understand that, but if you're counting on my people to save her, you're destined for disappointment. We have a large population of witches in Wilmington and the surrounding area. A lot more than you have. However, our purebloods died out a long time ago. We still have many who are quite talented, but there are also some who can barely perform basic parlor tricks. A few would be hard pressed to pull off a magic show at a kid's birthday party. It's simply not possible for us to beat the power of the amulet."

Their group is just like ours.

Alice tilted her head. "How do you know so much about our amulet?"

"Lucia kept a grimoire," Kara explained. "It's been passed down through my family since her death."

Deborah's eyes grew wide. "Oh, a spell book! I would sure love to see that."

"It's much more than a collection of spells." Kara sank back in her chair and crossed her legs. "She wrote about our people's history and even shared some of her visions. Since she sent the amulet with Charlotte, she created the grimoire to provide us with the knowledge contained within the amethyst. Well, as much of it as she could anyway."

Stevie stared at the floor for a long moment. In another set of circumstances, she would have sought more information about Lucia's book. But now, her thoughts revolved around Kara's bleak predictions regarding their inability to overpower Susan. She didn't think her situation could get any worse and yet, it had. And then there was Charlie. How could she begin to prepare him for life without a mother?

Stevie pursed her lips as she rose from her chair. "Let's talk strategy."

"I think it's best if the coven members stand with you. We'll form the front line," Dylan said. "We're all prepared to fight."

"Realistically, though, we might only be able to distract Susan." Randy rubbed his neck. "We had so little effect on her the night that she...killed Patricia."

"I don't want you to do anything. If you fight, she *will* kill you." Stevie's chest tightened at the thought of her coven facing Susan again. "Just be there. That's your only duty."

"I can't do that, Stevie." Dylan glanced at his fellow coven members. "None of us can."

Stevie made sure to look him in the eye. "You *have* to. The other witches from town will be there too. You have to set a good example for them. Those who want to help can cast a protection spell for me. It's a long shot, but it's better than nothing."

"The moon will be full that night. Susan will be at her most powerful," Deborah said.

Ruth clenched her fist. "And so will we."

"I know a good protection spell." Alice raised her eyebrows, hopeful. "The witnesses can chant together to combine their power to help protect Stevie."

Stevie shook her head. "No chanting. They'll have to remain silent or else Susan will know they're working with me."

"Perhaps it will still work if they only say it in their heads..." Alice wrung her hands.

Kara uncrossed her legs and leaned forward, resting her palms on her knees. "It won't be enough to protect you. You're going to have to find a way to eliminate Susan. Otherwise, this will never end."

"She's right." Ruth let out a heavy sigh. "Can we have another group focused on amplifying Stevie's power?"

"Yes, I like that. One group for power and one for protection," Lexi said.

Stevie remained quiet for moment, considering the strategy. "As long as their help isn't visible to Susan, I'll accept it."

Deborah eyed Kara. "Since Stevie has devised a strategy to protect the witnesses, will you bring your people?"

"I agree that this plan has reduced the likelihood of additional bloodshed, but you need to understand the other risk my people would take in coming here," Kara said. "If our group is revealed to Susan, what's going to stop her from trying to subjugate us too? My people rely on me to keep them safe. If I bring them here, they risk both death and discovery."

Kyle raised his head and locked eyes with Stevie. "I'll come. Can I join you on the front line?"

"Yes, of course." Stevie gave him a half smile. "Thank you."

Kara cut a sideways glance at her brother. "I'll come too, but I won't force my people to attend. I will *allow* them the option to come if they so choose."

"That's all I can ask," Stevie said.

Kara rose from her chair. "We're going to leave now. We'll see you at Cape Lookout on Saturday night."

Stevie stood as well. "I'll walk you out."

Kyle made no effort to move; instead, he turned to Lexi and began a discussion Stevie couldn't hear.

Kara glanced at her brother and issued an exasperated sigh. "Come on, Kyle."

"I want to show you something before you leave." Stevie led her guests toward the bottom of the staircase. "This is a portrait of Charlotte, Catherine, and Hannah." She pointed to the painting. "They allowed themselves to be captured by Blackbeard, facing unknown dangers. They left behind their families and friends, came here, and started over with nothing. They did this for the good of their people. *All* of their people."

Kara eyed the portrait for a moment but didn't say anything.

Chapter twenty-four

Stevie

The next morning, Stevie stepped out onto her front porch, coffee mug in hand. The cloudless sky allowed the sun's rays to shine unfettered, warming the air with its kiss. Fighting against the tightness in her chest, she drew in a deep breath and held it for a long moment.

Stevie spotted the yellow lab curled up near the porch steps, his belly still fat from the leftover ham she'd given him the night before.

She checked his water bowl and discovered that it was almost empty. Stevie made a mental note to refill it for him. The dog blinked and raised his head, gazing at her with curiosity. She bent down to pat his head.

"Good morning, Buddy." Stevie smiled as his tail thumped against the wooden slats of the porch floor. There were a few white hairs beneath his mouth, hardly noticeable against his pale, golden fur. She couldn't guess his age, but she suspected that he had several years under his belt. "If you're going to stick around, I guess I should invest in some dog food. Maybe I'll even let you sleep inside." He wagged his tail some more.

The front door opened and Dylan emerged from the house. He took a sip from his steaming cup of coffee as he joined Stevie at the porch railing.

He kissed the top of her head. "I see Lexi replenished the salt line last night."

Stevie turned to see for herself. The line of sea salt Lexi had traced around the house was at least three times thicker than it had been, and it was even wider at the door. "I guess she means business."

"She's just worried for you. We all are." Dylan stroked her back.

"What would happen if Susan tried to cross the salt line?" Stevie asked.

"It acts like a shield, sort of an invisible brick wall. She wouldn't be able to enter the house."

"I wish we'd thought of this earlier." Stevie nodded toward the salt. Her stomach churned with the memory of the night Susan had been in her home disguised as Dylan. "If it really does prevent anyone with ill-intent from entering, maybe we should use it all the time."

"I think they did in the old days, back when magic wasn't feared. But now, a ring of salt around a house is a dead give-away that a witch lives there."

"Oh, right. I guess that makes sense." She eyed the still, glassy water of Taylor's creek. "What do you think of Kara and Kyle? He seems okay, but I'm having trouble figuring her out. What are they thinking?"

"I can't read either of their thoughts. They use a mental shield just like you do. I suspect they have mind readers in Wilmington too."

They stood together in companionable silence for a while, sipping their coffees. A brown dog of indeterminate breed passed by Stevie's yard. He stopped when he reached the walkway, taking a moment to sniff the air, and then he continued down the street.

"I've been thinking about Saturday night." Dylan scratched the stubble on his jawline. "Do you really think the plan will work?"

"Honestly?" Stevie sighed. "No. I don't see how I can beat Susan, even with the help of protection and amplifying spells—but I have to try *something*."

He gulped. "I know the feeling."

"Lexi's going to take Charlie tomorrow. Today might be my last day with him." She pursed her lips and tightened her grip on her coffee mug. "I think we should do something fun. How about a visit to Carrot Island?"

"That sounds good. It's almost warm enough to swim."

"I think the water will be too chilly for that. Besides, Charlie will be content to play on the shore." She thought of the countless times she'd watched her son scoop the sand in his hand, only to let it stream out of his closed fist. He'd always loved the sensation of the granules brushing across his palm.

Dylan nodded. "How did Sam take the news that Charlie can't stay with him this weekend?"

"He didn't like it, that's for sure, especially since he missed last weekend. I had to lie to him, of course. I hate doing that." She fiddled with the hem of her shirt. "I told him that we're spending the weekend with my dad to try to help boost his spirits. That's something he wouldn't try to talk me out of."

"I know that was tough on you, but I don't see how you had a choice."

"I'll go visit my dad later today or tomorrow morning—maybe both." Stevie's voice cracked. "I want to see him one more time. I need to make sure he knows that I love him."

Stevie steered her skiff toward the dock. As she landed it with ease, Dylan grabbed the thick rope and tied it to the piling.

She glanced at Charlie, whose cheeks were pink from the sun, and sighed. They'd had a fun outing, exactly the type of day she wanted him to have—one he would remember long after she was gone. She stood by his side as he removed his life jacket and headphones, resisting the urge to provide unnecessary help. *He can do it all by himself.* She swallowed against the lump in her throat.

Dylan grabbed their cooler as he stepped off the skiff. Once on the dock, he offered his free hand to help them out of the boat.

Together, they walked across the street to Stevie's home. She opened the door, allowing Charlie to enter first.

"Charlie, go on up to your room. I'll be there in a few minutes to help you with your bath."

As soon as her son had climbed the stairs, she whirled back toward Dylan. "Would you mind going back to your own place after dinner tonight? I'd like to have some time alone with Charlie." She didn't dare to voice her other reason for wanting to be alone that night.

"Of course." Dylan stroked her arm. "If you need me, you'll call, right?"

"Yes." She tried to force a smile and failed.

"I know this is a terrible situation, and I can't imagine what you're going through right now." He clasped his hands around hers. "But if the worst should come to pass, I'll find a way to stay in Charlie's life. I love him too, you know. He won't want for anything."

Tears of gratitude pooled in Stevie's eyes. She had no doubt that Dylan meant what he had said. "Thank you," she whispered.

He drew his hands up, cupping her cheeks. "I love you, Stevie. I always have and I always will." He pressed his lips against hers.

****

In spite of the late hour, Stevie was unwilling to send Charlie to bed. Her heightened senses allowed her to hear his pulse, a steady beat just out of sync with her own. It reminded her that in spite of the deep connection they shared, he remained separate from her. Her death did not herald his. He could go on without her.

He will *go on without me.*

She wished she could stay snuggled up with him on the couch forever, inhaling the scent of his shampoo and listening for the words he might say next. But this night wasn't about her, it was about Charlie. As much as she wanted to spend every last moment with him, she knew she still had a lot to do. If she didn't survive her encounter with Susan, she wanted to make sure his transition to life without her went as smoothly as possible.

"All right, Charlie." She took in a deep breath in a futile effort to fight the heaviness in her heart. "Time for bed."

The boy rose from the couch and began to walk toward the stairs, with Stevie following close behind. She watched his smooth, bare feet as they ascended each wooden step with a soft pat. His knit pajama bottoms revealed an inch or two of his ankle. He'd only had those pajamas for a couple of months and they were already too short for him.

He's growing up fast. She blinked back the swell of tears that formed in her eyes and followed him to the upstairs bathroom.

She waited for him to brush his teeth and then tucked him into bed. "Did you have a good day?"

He nodded.

She stroked his cheek. "You know I love you, right?"

He nodded again.

"Always remember that." She leaned over and kissed his forehead. "Good night."

With a knot in her stomach, she made her way back downstairs. *It's time to get my affairs in order.*

Stevie plodded into her den, heading straight for the file drawer beneath her desk. She flipped through the folders until she located a copy of her will and skimmed over the document. It was all very straightforward. The house and all of her worldly possessions would go to Charlie. Her share of Coastal Visions, or at least what was left of it, would go to Lexi. Satisfied that she held the most current edition, she placed it on her desk.

She grabbed a piece of paper from the printer and began to list the contact information for Charlie's speech therapist, his pediatrician, and his teacher. Her hand trembled as she thought of all the information she wanted to share. His favorite pajamas. His preferred snack. A reminder to cut the tags off his clothes. She set her pen down and wiped away her tears.

Sam will figure it out. He has to.

She hoped that Lexi wouldn't have to keep Charlie hidden for very long. In spite of the differences she'd had with Sam, he was a good father. She wanted them to be together after she was gone. *He'll need his dad.*

She reached back into the file drawer and began seeking the paperwork for a small insurance policy that she'd taken out the year before. It wasn't much, but it should cover her final expenses—assuming Susan left anything to bury. She found it and added it to the stack of papers on her desk.

Stevie also plucked the title to her car from another file folder. *That might come in handy too.*

She tidied the pile of paperwork and left it in clear view on her desk. Sam or her dad should be able to find it easily.

And when they do, they'll know that I was planning to die.

Stevie let out a frustrated sigh and stuffed the papers into the front folder of her file drawer. *This will be the first place they'll look.*

Realizing she still had to finish writing her letter to Charlie, she pressed her hand against her aching chest. She couldn't bring herself to write it. *Later. I'll do it later.*

Stevie walked out of the den and down the length of the hallway, stopping when she reached the closet. When she pulled the door open, her gaze fell to the safe on the floor.

"You may not be strong enough to manage that much magic yet. The results could be catastrophic." Alice's warning rang in her ears.

But what choice did she have? Absorbing Vanessa's magic might very well be the only thing that could save her people from living under Susan's rule.

Or it might kill her.

Chapter twenty-five

Vanessa

"Fix me another one!" Susan bellowed as she waved her glass, sending an ice cube careening across the deck. "And get one for yourself while you're at it. I'm tired of drinking alone."

And I'm tired of watching you drink.

Vanessa trudged across the deck and collected the glass from her mother, who was once again lounging on her favorite chaise. Without a word, she descended the steps to the cabin and walked straight to the bar.

She knew that her mother was fully capable of conjuring up any beverage she desired. In fact, if she wanted to, she could probably cast a spell to send herself into inebriated oblivion, sparing herself the calorie hit. Vanessa clenched her jaw. *It's all about control.*

She placed the stout highball glass on the bar and selected a second one for herself. Vanessa had never been much of a drinker, but she had to do as her mother commanded. The two square ice cubes she dropped into the glass clinked against the thick crystal before settling at the bottom. She grabbed the half-empty bottle of bourbon and poured a generous serving of the golden brown liquid.

With any luck, this would be the drink that knocked her mother out. Drunk Susan was no fun at all, but a passed out Susan was at least tolerable. She began to pour again, doubling the volume of bourbon in the glass. *There...that should do it.*

Vanessa poured a modest serving for herself. She breathed in the deceptively sweet vanilla scent of the liquor and then took a sip. Warm and rich, it hit her mouth with a surprising bite she enjoyed. Humming a soft tune, she added a little more to her own glass as well.

Drinks in hand, she walked back out onto the deck. Her mother accepted the bourbon without a word of thanks. Vanessa stifled a sneer as she took a seat at the table.

"Everything is ready, you know." Susan stared out onto Front Street. She took an indelicate gulp of her bourbon and leaned back against the chaise's headrest. "Nothing left to do now but wait."

Vanessa sipped her drink. "Have you given any thought to what you want to do after the witches learn that you are their queen?"

She knew it wouldn't be enough for the witches to recognize Susan as their queen. Her mother would never be satisfied with the mere acquisition of power. She would have to exercise her control over her subjects, just as she'd done to Vanessa.

"As a matter of fact, I have." Susan smirked. "It's time for our people to come out of the shadows. We'll let the whole world know who we are and what we can do."

Vanessa's eyes grew wide. "But that will cause widespread witch hunts!"

"This time, we'll fight back." Susan indulged in another generous swig of her bourbon.

"People will die."

Susan tilted her head, meeting Vanessa's shocked stare. "That's a sacrifice I'm willing to make."

In ancient times, their people were revered, but far too much had changed since then. Vanessa couldn't imagine the world returning to a time when witches were free to practice their magic without condemnation. She had to admit it sounded like paradise though—provided her own powers were intact.

Susan drained her glass. She placed it on the small table at her side and then picked up her binoculars. "It's quiet over there tonight. Stevie sent the boyfriend away earlier. It's just her and the kid in there now."

Vanessa raised an eyebrow. "Can I get you another drink, Mother?"

Vanessa struggled to get Susan to her room. Barely conscious, her mother contributed little help with the process. If anything, her flailing limbs only impeded their progress down the narrow hall of the yacht.

Susan reeked of bourbon, leading Vanessa to wonder how the older witch's liver could withstand the abuse she heaped on it. *Probably her own special brand of binge drinking magic.*

When they finally reached the bed, she released her mother's dead weight, allowing her to tumble with an undignified plop onto the pillow top mattress. Susan let out a low groan as Vanessa pulled the plush comforter up to her shoulders.

Within a minute or two, Susan would lose consciousness altogether. Then Vanessa would be free to run her errand. She waited by her mother's side for a moment before she began to back out of the room.

Just as she reached the doorway, Susan spoke. "My daughter." Her voice was soft, lacking the harsh edge it usually carried.

Was it possible that Susan had gotten herself drunk enough to say something nice?

Vanessa froze. "Yes?"

Susan opened one eye, just a bit, and stared in Vanessa's general direction. "You sure are hideous!" She let out a loud cackle before her eye closed and her face went slack.

Vanessa scowled as she crept closer to Susan. Her gaze locked on the enormous amethyst pendant—the singular solution to all of her problems. She extended her hand toward it, wanting nothing more than to remove it from her sleeping mother's body. She caught herself before she touched it. If Susan had any sort of protection spell on the amulet, she would know Vanessa had tried to take it from her. She snapped her hand back to her side.

There's another way.

She went to her own cabin and snatched a couple of bobby pins from her dresser before stepping out onto the deck. Drawing in a deep breath of salt air, she set out to take back her power.

As she walked toward Stevie's house, she ran various scenarios through her mind. Stevie and the boy would likely be asleep at this hour, allowing her ample time to search the house for the safe that held her powers. Ideally, she'd find an unsecured door or window in order to gain entry, but if not, she had bobby pins to use on the door lock. She hoped the lock picking process was as straightforward as it appeared to be in the online tutorial she'd watched.

Vanessa clamped her hand on her stomach, trying to quell the nervous energy that fluttered within her. She'd be a fool not to acknowledge the inherent danger of breaking into that house again. Last time, Stevie had almost succeeded in killing her while she tried to get away. What would she do to her if she caught her now?

Vanessa cringed when she remembered the candle she'd left for the new queen. As far as Stevie knew, Vanessa had promised her loyalty. But that was *before* Susan promised to heal her burns. She wanted her scars gone just as much as she wanted her magic back.

She stood in front of Stevie's house. The curtains on the front windows were open, revealing the darkened rooms within. A dim, yellow glow came from somewhere near the back of the house. The kitchen, perhaps?

She crept closer, easing up the porch steps, and warily eyed the two bowls near the door. One was empty, the other contained water. She hadn't noticed them when she dropped off the candle just a few days earlier. She stole a quick glance around the yard in search of any new pets. The last thing she needed right now was a barking dog.

Finding the coast clear, she stepped onto the porch and made her way to one of the windows. Before she reached it, something else caught her eye. A thick line of salt extended across the doorstep. She didn't have to check the sides or the back to know that the salt line encircled the entire house.

161

Using salt to ward off evil was one of the oldest forms of magic known. Simple, yet effective. Vanessa backed away. She'd come to steal from Stevie—she would never be able to cross that line. Her shoulders slumped in disappointment. If she left now, no one ever had to know that she had come. She pivoted, ready to run away, only to find the owner of the bowls waiting for her at the bottom of the steps.

The yellow dog growled and bared his sharp teeth. His head angled upward as he looked her straight in the eye. She froze in place. The mutt blocked her exit. She searched frantically for another way out. But there was nowhere to go. Even if she managed to jump over the railing at the far end of the porch, he could be on her in no time.

"Easy, fella," she whispered.

He barked in reply.

"Shh!" Vanessa drew her finger to her mouth as if that would quiet him. A cold sweat broke out on her forehead. *I'm trapped.*

Suddenly, the front door swung open behind her. Vanessa spun around, heart racing, to find Stevie standing in the doorway.

"What the hell do you want?" Stevie's cheeks burned red with fury.

The dog quieted down, but Vanessa felt his presence behind her as she faced Stevie. Pinned between the two, she opted to try to talk to the one who at least spoke her language.

"My mother is going to kill you."

"I know. She pretty much told me so." Stevie's eyes narrowed. "Is that why you're here? To tell me something I already know?"

"There's something else…"

"Go ahead, spit it out. You know I don't have much time left. Don't waste any more of it."

"She's going to kill Charlie too." The words left a foul taste in Vanessa's mouth.

Stevie held her chin high, but her tone softened. "I was afraid of that."

"I think I know how she's going to do it." Vanessa own words shocked her. She hadn't planned to share any details with Stevie, but the sight of her—of Charlie's mother—had impacted her in a way she could not have predicted.

Vanessa resisted the urge to squirm under the weight of Stevie's glare. As the yellow dog behind her and the fierce witch before her continued with their silent assessments, she wondered if she would make it back to the yacht alive.

Stevie glanced down at the salt line in front of the door and then raised her head, locking eyes with Vanessa once more. "Why don't you come in so we can discuss this further?"

Vanessa had a decision to make.

Chapter twenty-six

Stevie

Friday passed too quickly. By nightfall, the full coven had assembled in Stevie's kitchen, completing their preparations for the next day.

Alice had placed two bags of stones on the table. "I brought all of the moonstones and amber I had." After selecting one stone from each bag, she held up a milky white gem for all to see. "We'll pass these out among the solitary witches who are helping with the power spell. We don't have enough for all of them, so try to make sure the weaker witches have one first." She held up the piece of golden resin that she had selected from the other bag. "Same thing with the amber. These will help with the protection spell."

"Can we do a protection spell for Charlie? If Susan is watching when he leaves tonight…" Stevie stifled a shudder.

Deborah's knitting needles clicked as her row of white yarn expanded across her blanket. "Already done, dear."

"Thank you." The news did nothing to quell the knot of anxiety that twisted in Stevie's stomach. She glanced at Lexi. "It's getting late. You're probably ready to get on the road."

Lexi placed her hand on Stevie's shoulder and flashed a sweet smile. "Don't worry about me. We'll leave when *you're* ready."

Certain she'd never be ready to send Charlie away to an unknown location for an unknown amount of time, she couldn't hold Lexi's gaze. "Come with me."

Lexi followed her out of the kitchen and into the den. They stopped at Stevie's desk.

"Everything you need for the shop is in here." Stevie pulled open the file drawer and pointed to a folder labeled "Coastal Visions." Then she pointed to a file in front of the drawer. "This one has my will and other information that my dad and Sam will need."

Lexi's eyes grew wide. "You're planning to die, aren't you?"

"I'll fight with everything I have, but we have to be realistic about this." Stevie closed the file drawer. "I don't see how I can beat her, but if I don't make it, I'll die knowing I did everything I could to ensure the safety of my people."

Lexi let out a long hitched breath. "What am I supposed to tell Sam and your dad?"

"I guess that depends on what's left of me." Stevie grimaced. "Randy should be able to come up with a relatively reasonable explanation. It's not the first time he's had to tackle that responsibility." Her stomach churned at the thought of her mother's murder.

"Lexi?" Dylan entered the room carrying a small duffle bag. "Take this with you."

Lexi's brow furrowed. "What is it?"

"Cash. Don't use any credit cards or checks while you're away." Dylan handed the bag to her. "She may still be able to track you down with magic, but if not, this will help."

The thought of Susan finding them sent a chill racing up Stevie's spine. This may all be for nothing, but she sure as hell wasn't going to make it easy for the dark witch to get to her son.

"As soon as it's safe, bring him back to Sam." Stevie bit down on her quivering lip.

Tears pooled in Lexi's eyes. "And what if it's never safe?"

"That's not going to happen." Dylan clenched his jaw. "We'll find a way to stop her."

Stevie had always hated goodbyes, but this was, by far, the worst she'd ever endured. Lexi and Dylan stood by Lexi's car, having already loaded the bag of cash and Charlie's suitcase into the trunk. Stevie waited on the porch while Charlie knelt down to give Buddy a loving pat on the head. The dog's tail wagged in enthusiastic appreciation. Then he rose to his feet and licked Charlie's face, sending her son into a fit of giggles the likes of which she had never seen before. She burst into laughter, forgetting her anguish for a brief moment.

Her smile faded almost the instant it appeared. Charlie was growing and changing so fast. She didn't want to miss a minute of it. A wave of dizziness struck, and she gripped the porch railing to steady herself.

This is his best chance.

Stevie straightened her back. "It's time to go." She forced her quaking voice to sound cheerful. As far as Charlie knew, he would be going on a fun adventure with Lexi.

The nearly full moon outshone the stars in the sky. When they reached Lexi's car, Stevie knelt down, putting herself at eye level with her son. "Have fun, Charlie. I will—" She cut herself off. She'd almost said that she would see him soon. She blinked. Grateful for the darkness of the night that hid the pain in her eyes. "I will miss you."

Stevie brushed her hand along his soft cheek, studying his cherubic face. When his fleeting glance met hers, she smiled.

He's going to be okay. He has to be okay.

She ruffled his hair and kissed his forehead. "I love you."

Lexi and Dylan stepped away as they waited in silence for Stevie to say her goodbye.

"Let's get you buckled up." Stevie opened the back door of the car. Charlie climbed in and settled into his seat. She fastened his seat belt, giving it a firm tug to make sure he was secure.

Charlie furrowed his brow. *He's probably picking up on my sadness.* But there was nothing more that she could tell him now. The truth was too terrifying. Anything else would be a lie. She could only give him a reassuring smile.

The sound of Buddy's frantic barking cut through the stillness of the moment. Stevie whirled around to find Susan standing behind her. Icy tendrils of fear coursed through her veins. Instinctively, she remained in front of the open car door, blocking Susan's view of Charlie.

Stevie barely had a second to process Susan's arrival when Lexi suddenly lunged forward, jaw clenched and palms open. The white light of her magic had already begun to pool within her hand.

"Lexi, no!" Dylan reached for her arm, but he was too late. She'd already fired a pulse toward the dark witch.

Susan showed no fear, only annoyance at the interruption. She raised her hand and deflected Lexi's magic, sending it right back at her. The white light struck Lexi in the chest—and she hit the ground with a thud.

Stevie gasped and drew her hand to her mouth. "Lexi!" She wanted to run to her friend, but she couldn't bring herself to leave Charlie unprotected.

Dylan knelt down and placed two fingers on the side of Lexi's neck, searching for a pulse.

"I've been watching you all week." Susan sneered at Stevie. "Did you really think you could hide the kid without me knowing about it?"

Stevie's attention snapped back to the dark witch. The older members of the coven had assembled on the porch, helpless. She suspected that they too recalled the night they'd all tried to fight Susan. There had been no victory. Only death.

"He'll stay with me tonight." Susan locked her cold, dark eyes on Stevie. "That way I know you'll *both* be at my party tomorrow."

Stevie raised her hands in protest. "Please don't do this." She couldn't control the petrified quiver in her voice.

Susan bared her teeth. "If you try to come for the boy, I will kill him." In a flash, she disappeared as abruptly as she had appeared.

Stevie whipped back toward the car and reached for Charlie. But his seat was empty. Bile rose in her throat as she searched the vehicle, back and front. Frantic, she looked up and down the street. But there was no sign of him.

"No!" She clenched her fists and screamed.

Dylan raced to her side as she slumped, trembling, against the car. He wrapped his arm around her waist, steadying her. "I've got you."

Stevie's gaze fell to Lexi. Randy was already kneeling beside her. "Is she okay?" Hoarseness tinged her voiced.

Randy nodded. "She will be. I had no idea her magic was so powerful. She must have put everything she had into that strike." He glanced up at Dylan. "Help me take her inside before anyone sees us out here."

Dylan knelt beside Lexi's petite figure, lifted her with ease, and carried her into the house. Without a word, Deborah and Alice followed them.

Randy approached Stevie. "We have to get you inside too."

"No."

Randy inched closer, scanning the street for witnesses. "We have to—"

Stevie ground her teeth. "I need to go get Charlie!"

"You can't do that." Randy kept his voice calm and steady. "You know what she'll do."

Crackles of energy danced around her clenched fists. "She has my son."

Ruth rested her hand on Stevie's shoulder. "Come on. We'll talk about this inside."

They were right. She knew it. As much as she wanted to deny it, she had to comply. With reluctance, Stevie put one foot in front of the other, her chest tight with an agonizing combination of fear and rage. She heard Randy close the car door behind her. Together they walked toward her house. Her heart raced faster with each step. She wasn't walking toward her home. She was walking away from Charlie—farther and farther away from her little boy.

She crossed the threshold and heard the door click closed. Every ounce of strength that remained in her body dissipated. Her legs betrayed her, giving out with no warning. She dropped to her knees. "He must be so scared!"

Dylan rushed out of the living room, where he had placed Lexi on the couch. "I'll take care of Stevie," he said to Randy. "Lexi is starting to come to. Can you check on her?"

Randy stepped away, and Dylan helped Stevie to her feet. He pulled her close, holding her head against his chest.

She felt as though she were sinking, descending into madness. She wanted to scream. She wanted to fight. She wanted to kill.

The fury boiled within her, electrifying her whole body. She couldn't stay away from the yacht. Not with her baby on it.

"Come on." Dylan took her by the arm. "Let's go get you a drink."

Alice called from the kitchen. "Bring her back here. I have a tea that will calm her down."

Dylan walked with Stevie toward the kitchen and helped get her settled in a chair. "A tea isn't going to do it. She needs something a lot more potent than that."

"Trust me," Alice said. "This is *exactly* what she needs right now." She placed the steamy brew in front of Stevie on the table. "Drink up!"

Stevie heard the front door open and close, followed by the sound of Buddy's long claws clicking rapidly along the wooden floorboards of the hallway. His pace didn't slow until he arrived at her side.

Ruth entered the room behind the dog. "I had to let him in. Poor thing was worried sick about you."

Buddy rested his head on Stevie's knee. His deep brown eyes reflected the same pain she endured.

"Drink that tea while it's hot, Stevie." Alice wagged her finger. "It'll help you sleep."

Stevie shook her head. "There's no way I'm going to sleep tonight! Not as long as Susan has Charlie."

Dylan put his hand on her shoulder. "Please drink it, Stevie. There's nothing more you can do tonight. You need your rest, so you can get Charlie back tomorrow."

Stevie couldn't argue with that. She took a long sip of the hot tea. Alice had attempted to mask its pungent earthiness with a copious amount of honey, but bitterness lingered on her tongue in spite of its sweetness. She set the mug on the table and sat up straighter in her chair, still unaffected by its sedating ingredients.

Unable to contain the rage that consumed her, Stevie slammed her fist down on the kitchen table. "I'm going to kill that bitch!"

"That's right, dear." Alice nodded. "And we're going to help you do it."

Chapter twenty-seven

Stevie

Stevie continued to sip the tea Alice had made for her. She didn't enjoy the flavor, but it had been effective in settling her nerves. Her pulse slowed, and her breathing returned to something resembling normal. Buddy relinquished his spot on her knee in favor of curling up under the table at her feet. Conversation swirled around her, but she took no part in it.

"Do you think anyone saw what happened out there?" Dylan asked Alice.

"Surely not." The elder witch shook her head. "The police would have come by now if they had."

Stevie perked up when Randy and Deborah entered the kitchen. "How's Lexi?"

"Much better." Randy came to stand beside her. "How are *you* doing?"

"I'm okay, I guess." Stevie shrugged. "Alice's tea helped."

Randy nodded. "Good. Drink a little more."

Stevie glanced at her teacup and then back to Randy. "Will you try to look for Charlie tonight? In your dreams, I mean? I just need to know that he's safe. I need to know that he's not hurt." She bit down on her lip. "You'll tell me if you see anything, right?"

"Of course I will." Randy nudged the half-full teacup toward Stevie. "But please don't get your hopes up. I haven't had any visions involving Susan in quite some time. I think she knows about my gift and is somehow blocking me from seeing her. There's no telling how much she's learned about us from the amulet."

Stevie didn't attempt to mask her disappointment as she took another gulp of her tea. It warmed her body, but the chill in her soul remained.

The night grew longer. In one moment, Stevie thought she'd been in her kitchen for hours. The next, she thought perhaps only a few minutes had passed. She wasn't sure if she had lost her grip on time or if she'd somehow been released from its relentless forward motion. Though she sat among her beloved coven members in her own kitchen, she felt oddly disconnected. Exhaustion crept into bones, but she wasn't yet ready to give in to sleep. Her mind spun with murky memories that only served to bring her back to her sole concern—Charlie.

The tea had quelled the restlessness in her body, but it hadn't quieted her thoughts enough. Stevie recalled the first time she drank one of the special concoctions—the night of her induction into the coven. That particular brew had helped her view a clear vision of a long ago past. It had allowed her to stand alongside Lucia as a silent, invisible observer while she sacrificed her own daughter, along with Hannah and Catherine, during Blackbeard's raid of their private island home. Stevie recalled

Charlotte's clever plan to escape the *Queen Anne's Revenge*. Even as an untested queen, Charlotte had been successful in her endeavor, but not before the pirate had forced himself on Hannah. His violent act created a new family line in Beaufort, one that, generations later, produced Susan and all of the misery that she had wrought.

Susan is evil—and she has Charlie.

Then there was Vanessa's appearance on her doorstep the night before. She hadn't mentioned anything about Susan's plans to kidnap Charlie. Had she known it would happen?

Stevie blinked back anxious tears and tried to raise the teacup to her lips, but its weight had multiplied since she'd taken her first sip. If she couldn't rescue Charlie tonight, then she wanted to drink her way out of the hell she endured now. She forced herself to concentrate on raising her arm, but it had grown heavy as well. Despite her will, her arm refused to budge, and she let out a frustrated groan.

A familiar voice cut through her brooding. "Um, is she okay?"

She tilted her head upward to find Lexi standing beside her, frowning. Stevie's heart buoyed at the sight of her best friend back on her feet, but she couldn't bring herself to smile.

"I'm okay," Stevie tried to say, but she only managed to utter an unintelligible grunt.

A sudden flurry of movement began to bustle around her. Lexi faded away and Randy's face appeared before her, his brow crinkled in concentration. His image blurred into an incomprehensible swirl of white hair and wrinkles. She blinked in a futile attempt to focus her vision.

Randy stroked her cheek with his cool, soothing hand. "She'll be fine, but we need to get her upstairs—she needs to be in her bed."

Dylan stepped to her side. "Can you stand?" He reached for her hand, offering additional support.

Stevie exhaled, preparing herself for the effort it would take to rise from the chair she had melted into. She placed her free hand on the table. It wobbled and wiggled like a gel in her grasp before it solidified enough for her to gain purchase. She pushed herself up, managing to stay upright for only a second or two before falling into Dylan's arms.

Dylan grunted as he caught her. "I wouldn't have thought a cup of tea could do so much damage." He pulled her arm across his shoulders and wrapped his own arm around her waist. "She's smashed."

Deborah peeked into Stevie's mug. Her eyes widened with surprise. "She only drank about half of it." She threw a suspicious glance at Alice. "What did you put in it?"

Alice lifted the teacup from the table. "I made it a little stronger than usual. Perhaps a little too strong." She sniffed defensively. "It's an art, you know. Not a science."

Dylan began to steer Stevie out of the kitchen and toward the staircase as the conversation continued, fading away with each new step.

"I didn't know herbs could do all of this." Lexi's voice carried down the hall. "Not legal ones anyway."

"There's nothing illegal in that tea, I can assure you. But I may have added a little magic to it as well." Alice showed no hint of regret in her confession. "Our queen needs her rest. All of this stress is bad for her."

Supported by Dylan, Stevie stumbled along the hallway. The voices from the kitchen reduced to almost inaudible murmurs in the distance. When they reached the foyer, they stopped. They both stared up the length of the staircase, realizing at the same time that there was no way Stevie could make it to the top on her feet.

Dylan squeezed her arm. "Don't worry."

She didn't.

He scooped her up and began to climb the staircase. Stevie closed her eyes and imagined she was flying.

She must have dozed off for a moment because the next thing she became aware of was Dylan slipping her shoes off. She heard them fall to the floor as she lay on her bed. She giggled self-consciously as she felt him unbutton her jeans. Without a word, he slid them off her hips and down her legs with ease. Then he drew the blanket up to her shoulders.

"I've never loved anyone the way I love you, Stevie Lewis." He brushed her hair away from her face and leaned in, placing a gentle kiss on her forehead. "I will do whatever it takes to bring you and Charlie home tomorrow. Whatever it takes."

She mumbled something incoherent. It sounded nothing at all like the "I love you" she meant to say.

Stevie closed her eyes, surrounding herself with blackness. She began to fall, deeper and deeper into the abyss of sleep, and she surrendered willingly.

The dreams came right away, haunting her rest with her waking worries.

Stevie stood alone on her dock in the dark of night. The full moon marked the water as its own with a glistening reflection. A frigid wind cut through her thin sweater, raising gooseflesh on her skin. She folded her arms and shivered, wishing she had worn a jacket.

She became aware of a rising susurration as the cold wind increased its power, whistling and whispering. It gusted against her, hissing a single intelligible word. "Stevie."

She forgot the cold, but her gooseflesh remained.

"Stevie." The wind hit her again, sending its icy tendrils through her body and into her soul. She recognized its voice.

She saw movement out of the corner of her eye. A shadowy form zipped past her. Its tattered rags brushed her skin with a painful, biting freeze. She lost sight of it for an instant in the gloom. Stevie barely had time to process its absence when it appeared on her right side and then again on her left, taunting and terrifying. It darted back and forth before her, an endless swirl of chaos and madness.

It continued its macabre dance, inching closer to her with each pass. Stevie couldn't see its eyes or any other defining characteristic of the form. She only sensed the depth of its malevolence. It was almost upon her when, with a shriek like metal scraping metal, it shot up high into the night sky. It became a minute stain of black on black before diving back down and hurtling straight toward her. Paralyzed with fear, she could not move.

The shadowy form stopped just inches away from Stevie. She saw it clearly now. A grisly demon in a ragged black shroud. Its visage appeared deteriorated, rotting in its own evil.

"Stevie," it hissed her name with Susan's voice. The heat of its fetid breath grazed her cheek.

She opened her mouth to speak, only to find that her own voice had abandoned her along with her ability to move. With rising terror, she understood that the fiend held all of the power. She was helpless. Unable to run or fight, she would be subject to any horror it intended to dole out.

The evil spirit darted away, cackling as it flew.

A flash of light from above blinded Stevie for a moment. As soon as her eyes adjusted to the glare, she looked up and spotted a grouping of stars, brighter than the rest. They formed a constellation that began to resolve into the shape of a face. They morphed further still into the image of her mother—a wondrous, welcome vision. It faded away as quickly as it had appeared.

More flashes came and went, illuminating the night sky in a brilliant storm of familiarity. Her grandmother, Charlotte, and Lucia all appeared as well. More constellations revealed themselves to her. Though she did not recognize the current stream of images that flashed in the darkness, she somehow knew the women who now danced among the stars. They were her ancestors. Her family.

They were the queens who had come before her. A line of noble women. They were a part of her, and she was a part of them. The sight of their images fortified her. They reminded her of her heritage, her birthright, her responsibility. Stevie wanted to make them proud.

The demon reappeared suddenly in front of her, ripping her away from the comfort of her nostalgia. It stood nose to nose with her, raising its bony hand, metacarpals clicking as it moved. It rammed its skeletal finger into her chest, and its piercing shriek rang out in the night. "There can only be one queen!"

"There can only be one queen," the stars echoed in agreement as the demon raced away.

Chapter twenty-eight

Stevie

A hard rain drummed against the roof of Stevie's house on Saturday afternoon. Racked with worry, she leaned against the doorframe of Charlie's bedroom and stared at his empty bed—longing to hold her son in her arms.

Did he sleep last night? Did he have anything to eat? How did he communicate his needs without his tablet? Was he scared? She wrapped her arms around herself. *Is he as scared as I am?*

On and on it went, the vicious cycle of worry and gut-wrenching uncertainty that had plagued Stevie since she'd opened her eyes that morning. Upon waking, she had first been fearful as she remembered the unsettling dream she'd had. As that dream faded from her mind, the events of the previous night crashed back in on her. Fear gave way to devastation. At times, she felt it might devour her, searing through her body and soul until there was nothing left. Other times, her anger burned through the pain. That too held the potential to be all-consuming. She closed her eyes and shook her head. She had to stay strong. For Charlie. For her people.

Stevie backed away from Charlie's door and walked back her own room to collect the piece of sea glass. She picked it up from her dresser and rubbed her thumb along its matte finish before she slipped it into the pocket of her jeans.

Stevie descended the stairs to the foyer, pausing when she reached the portrait of Charlotte, Hannah, and Catherine. She looked into their eyes, seeking advice they could not give. Would she ever lay eyes on this portrait again? If Susan had her way, Stevie would meet these brave witches in person tonight—in the afterlife.

The front door opened behind her. Dylan emerged carrying the duffle bag of cash he'd stowed in Lexi's trunk the night before. Droplets of rain ran down his thick hair, falling onto his jacket. He unzipped the bag and removed a stack of one hundred dollar bills. He counted them and folded them over.

"What's that for?" Stevie asked.

"In case any non-witches are there and need encouragement to leave the area." He crammed the wad of bills into his pocket. "I don't know what Susan has planned, but I can guarantee it's not something we'd want the general population to witness."

"Good idea—but how will you explain what we're all doing out there?"

"People don't tend to ask a lot of questions when it's more profitable to remain silent," he said. "But if I have to say something, I guess I'll just tell them that we're having a private party."

"That should work." Stevie nodded, though she was certain the events of the evening would be anything but a party.

Dylan ran a hand through his soaked hair. "I doubt it will be much of an issue anyway. This rain will probably keep away the beachgoers and casual fishermen."

Stevie plucked her rain jacket from the hook beside the door and slipped into it. "Is everyone ready?"

"The coven members will ride over with us. They're all waiting on the porch now. The others will take their own boats, or catch a ride with friends, and meet us there."

"Okay." Stevie gulped. "Let's get this over with."

Dylan grabbed her hand and pulled her toward him. "Not yet."

He looked into her eyes, stopping time just for the two of them. She felt the stroke of his hand along her cheek and the depth of his love in his gaze. He did not say anything. He didn't need to. He leaned in, pressing his lips against hers. She welcomed the kiss. The moment lasted for always, and yet it was gone before she knew it.

They emerged from the house, joining the rest of the coven on the porch. She looked at each one of them, overwhelmed with gratitude. Deborah, Lexi, Ruth, Randy, Alice and Dylan were all ready to follow her into an unknown and dangerous future. They didn't tremble in fear at the thought of Susan's unpredictable rage. They stood ready to fight for their queen and her son. She loved them all, and she would do anything within her power to keep them safe.

She walked toward Dylan's dock, crossing the empty street in the rain, with her loyal coven following behind her. The sound of Buddy's bark caught her attention as they reached the dock. She whirled around to find the yellow lab racing to be by her side.

"Go back home, Buddy."

The dog didn't leave. He cocked his head toward Ruth instead.

"He wants to be with you." Ruth scratched his snout. "You're his person now."

Stevie shook her head. "He could get hurt!"

"Yeah, well, so could I." Ruth raised an eyebrow. "But I don't see you trying to send me back home."

"A lot of good that would do." Stevie smirked. "You wouldn't sit this out if I told you to."

"My point exactly."

"All right." Stevie glanced down at the dog with a defeated sigh. "You can come too." She gave his head a quick pat. "Good boy."

Dylan landed his boat on the sound side of Cape Lookout. Stevie saw no other vessels in the area, indicating a high probability that they would have the island to themselves. The rain had begun to ease up and had already reduced to little more than a sprinkle. She hoped it would come to a complete stop soon.

Stevie eyed the narrow strip of beach and decided to move the group to the ocean side of the island, where the broader expanse of sand would allow ample room for everyone. She led her coven across a wooden walkway which extended over the dunes and greenery that made up the center of the island.

They waited on the soft sand for the others to arrive. Stevie began to pace, and Buddy followed her as if he had been trained to do so. The lighthouse stood tall behind them, flashing its light every fifteen seconds now that it had been released from the magical spell.

The sun hung low in the sky, supplying a little warmth before it retired for the day. As the clouds began to part and the drizzle came to a stop, other witches from town began to join them on the beach. Some came alone, while others joined them in groups. Stevie welcomed her people and made a point to speak to each one as they arrived.

"Thank you for coming." She moved from one to the other, solemn and sincere, greeting each witch just like she would a fellow mourner at a wake.

They came from all parts of Beaufort. Some she knew by name, others she did not. Most were familiar to her in some way. She'd seen them at Charlie's school, or at Backstreet Pub, or had passed them in a grocery store aisle at some point. Men and women, some possessed the fresh faces of youth; others had the gray hairs that came with life experience. They were all her people, her responsibility. Stevie took small comfort in the knowledge that the children and elderly, the most vulnerable of her kind, had remained safe in their homes. Susan couldn't get to them. Not tonight anyway.

Kara and Kyle arrived. Though Stevie's heart sank at the realization that they'd come alone, she welcomed them. "Thank you for coming."

Kara's dark hair fluttered in the breeze as she eyed the growing number of witches who congregated along the beach. "Have there been any changes to the plan?" She didn't volunteer an explanation regarding the absence of her people.

"No." Stevie shook her head. "It's still my hope that everyone will emerge from this alive and well. However, I believe my coven will probably fight on my behalf in spite of my protests."

"I'm not surprised. They have great respect for you." Kara's lip twitched with the slightest flash of a smile, offering an uncharacteristic flicker of warmth. "That much is obvious."

Kyle remained at Kara's side, his long hair tied in a ponytail. He kept his arms folded across his thick chest as he scanned the area. To Stevie, he acted more like a bodyguard than a brother.

More and more witches from town gathered on the beach. Stevie drew her hand to her mouth, overwhelmed by the sight of all of them together. A few had started small fires along the shore, and now they huddled around them for warmth. She recalled Lexi's unique method of starting a fire without wood. She wondered how these solitary witches, whom she knew so little about, managed to get their own fires going. Had they produced their flames with only a well-focused thought? Or, had they clutched a gemstone and recited an old spell? If Stevie had learned anything in recent weeks, it was that magical techniques varied from witch to witch.

The parted clouds revealed the orange hues of a typical fall sunset. On any other day, Stevie would have reveled in that glorious sight. She might have taken pictures of it or just watched the sun drop from the sky. Either way, she would have enjoyed the experience, marveling at the wonder of the world.

But this day was different. *No time for that now.* When the sun sank out of sight, the moon would soon take its place—and when the moon arrived, so would Susan.

She'll bring Vanessa too. Stevie swallowed hard and pressed against the knot of anxiety that twisted in her stomach.

Deborah approached and draped her arm across Stevie's shoulders. "How are you doing?"

Stevie sighed. "Okay, I guess. Tough day."

"I know, sweetie. Your mother would be so proud of you. Remember that." She gave Stevie's shoulder a squeeze. "Take a moment and watch this gorgeous sunset. Collect your thoughts. You'll need to speak to your troops soon."

My troops. How had her life changed so much in such a short time? It seemed like only yesterday she was taking snapshots on Carrot Island to sell in her shop. Now, her store had been destroyed, and she was in the process of preparing the magically inclined residents of Beaufort for the possibility of battle.

Deborah strolled away, leaving Stevie alone to contemplate what she would say to the witches who'd assembled on her behalf. She watched the sun dip below the horizon and allowed herself to relish its beauty. Yes, today was different. Today was the day she *should* watch the sun set. *I may never have another opportunity to do so.*

Red and orange hues gave way to shades of violet and blue. Stevie's trepidation only increased at the sight of the ever-darkening sky. The moon would soon rise, bringing Susan's lunacy along with it.

The time had come to address her people. She had to at least try to prepare them for what might happen.

She turned to the gathering of more than two hundred witches. As though by instinct, they abandoned their individual conversations and gave their full attention to their queen. They stood several deep between Stevie and the sand dunes, stretched out along the beach. The wind blew against her back, and she hoped it would carry her voice for all to hear.

She drew in a deep breath, filling her lungs with the salty ocean air. As she exhaled, she looked up to address her people.

"Tonight, Susan Moore will claim that she is your queen. She is not. I am, by blood and by birth. More than that, I'm your queen because I've accepted the responsibility of protecting you. I do this out of love—not because I seek any special privilege or power." She paused, considering her next words. "I can't say the same for Susan's intentions. She presents a danger unlike any we've ever encountered before. It's true that she killed my mother and stole the amulet. It's also true that her amplified power is more than enough to overcome our combined efforts."

Stevie waited for a response from the crowd. Nothing she'd said was different from what her coven members had already shared with the solitary witches, so there were no murmurs of surprise among the group. They all stood at attention, ready to take instructions from their queen. She noticed Maura, Charlie's teacher, in the crowd. Stevie nodded in acknowledgement as she caught her eye.

"You already know that Susan plans to kill me tonight." Stevie willed her voice to stay steady enough to relay the rest of her statement. "In addition to that, she kidnapped my son last night."

She heard several gasps come from the assembled crowd. Her gaze shifted to Maura, whose hand now covered her mouth. "Susan is ruthless and cruel. I'll stop at nothing to save my son and my people from her."

The men and women who stood before her nodded their heads in agreement.

"You need to know that she will kill anyone who tries to stop her. That includes anyone who tries to help me." Stevie held her chin high. "My priority as your queen is to keep you safe. I don't want you to put yourselves in danger for me. You can help, however, by discreetly casting protection and power spells. Alice and Deborah will help you get organized. Remember to hide your efforts when Susan arrives. As far as she knows, you're here only to witness whatever display of power she plans to show you tonight."

Alice and Deborah moved in front of the crowd, each holding a bag of gemstones. They began to gather participants and separate them into groups.

"Do we have any healers here?" Stevie asked.

Randy stepped forward and stood by Stevie's side. Two more men and three women emerged from the crowd. They joined Stevie and Randy.

"I hope we don't need any of your gifts tonight, but we should be prepared for anything. Before Susan arrives, I want one or two of you to hide behind the dunes. If things go really bad, it'll be good to have healers waiting in the wings." Stevie pointed to the mounds of sand beyond the gathering of witches. "I want the rest of you to spread out. Be ready to help if necessary."

Randy and his crew nodded. Randy gave Stevie's arm a squeeze. "Good job."

Stevie spoke to the full assembly of witches again. "When I...*if* I should fall tonight, you must continue your efforts of self-preservation. I don't know what Susan's long term plans are, but I know I want you all to survive."

A thick lump grew in her throat as the love she possessed for her people threatened to overwhelm her. She recalled the wave of emotion that had washed over her following the death of her mother. Even in the absence of the amulet, Stevie had inherited the queen's devotion. She had come to believe that it was some sort of genetic trait that had helped ensure the survival of her kind for thousands of years. Was it the same for the other witches? Did they care for her as she cared for them?

"Now that you know the full scope of the situation, I invite you to leave if that's your choice. You don't have to stay here."

No one moved. There were no chatters of discussion among the witches. Stevie bit her lip as she took in the sight. Of course they all stayed. These were citizens of Beaufort, where people helped their neighbors. They looked after each other. One was always ready with a kind word, a casserole, or even a protection spell if that's what the circumstances called for.

"Okay then. You all have your assignments. Please get started. Remember, *do not let her see you help me*. Protect yourselves first."

Stevie walked the stretch of beach, observing, while preparations began. With Buddy at her side, she watched as Deborah and Alice finished dividing the assembled witches into two groups—one to focus on protection, the other on power. They distributed the gemstones to the weaker witches first.

Deborah raised her arms as though she were conducting a choir. At her direction, her group began chanting first. "Protection. Protection. Protection."

Nearby, Alice's group chimed in next. "Power. Power. Power."

Their voices thrummed a steady beat against the sound of waves crashing ashore. Vigorous, haunting, and devastatingly beautiful.

Chapter twenty-nine

Stevie

The full moon had already begun its almost impercep-
tible rise. Stevie stood yards away from the water's
edge, her back to the dunes and the groups of witches who
had come to support her. They continued their chants, filling
her with all of the magic and protection they could muster.
Now that they'd settled into it, their songs had developed an
effortless rhythm. Their combined power swelled within her as
the air around her seemed to solidify, creating a thick shield of
invisible armor.

Dylan stood at her left side and Lexi at her right. Deborah,
Alice, Ruth, Randy, Kara, and Kyle stretched out on either side
of them, forming the front line. Buddy sat in front of her, vigilant, his ears perked up. His tail swept a smooth arc in the sand.

The ocean, blackened by the night, sent its waves ashore
with unceasing fury. White caps crashed on the sand, only to
draw back into the murky depths and roar forward once again.
The wind carried the waves' essence to Stevie, blowing her hair
away from her face and peppering her with a salty spray. She
breathed it all in, pulling the ocean's power into herself.

Stevie knew she needed to lower the mental shield that she employed to prevent Dylan from reading her thoughts. She couldn't afford to expend her energy on anything other than protecting her people from Susan. Her magic, though multiplied now, still had its limits, and her body had a finite capacity to contain it all. She'd waited as long as she could in an effort to hide her secret from Dylan.

She recalled pulling the safe from the closet and squeezed her eyes closed. *Dylan will be furious.*

She focused on the white light of her mental shield and envisioned it dissolving, freeing her mind and her magic. As soon as it disappeared, she focused on the gifts coming from the witches assembled behind her, accepting their chanted offerings of power and protection with gratitude.

Stevie patted the sea glass that lay nestled in her pocket and considered all that it represented. Earth, air, fire, and water—all of the elements of her kingdom.

The ocean, her ocean, with its boundless energy, lay before her. A force unto itself, it had the power to both terrorize and mesmerize. At once vicious and serene, it was a killer and a healer.

Though multiple sources of magic surrounded her, the one that commanded her notice the most was love. Her love for her people and their love for her. It had become a fount of unending power and hope. It forced her to face the horrors that Susan wrought head-on, and it kept her steady as she stood on the brink of an unthinkable future. She pressed her hand against her chest as her heart swelled with devotion.

A sudden gust of wind kicked up, spewing sand against the assembly of witches and extinguishing their fires. Lightning ripped through the sky overhead—first one bolt, then another. A fierce rumble of thunder shook the earth beneath her feet. Stevie looked to the sky. There were no clouds overhead, only the bright, full moon and its accompanying stars. But a storm brewed nonetheless—one that her people would never forget.

The chanting ceased. In the prevailing silence, Stevie knew that they too awaited the oncoming tempest. Buddy rose to his feet, hackles up and ears forward. He let out a low growl.

"Stay quiet, boy." She kept her voice low.

Another radiant bolt of lightning flashed. This time, it struck near the surf, blinding Stevie for a moment. She blinked away the spots in her field of vision. By the time her eyes adjusted, three forms had appeared on the compacted sand at the water's edge.

Susan's long black skirt billowed in the ocean wind. She did not speak. Instead, her fierce glare raked across the crowd. Vanessa stood to her right, wearing the same hoodie Stevie had seen her in before. Susan had positioned Charlie in front of herself, like a shield. With a bony hand clutching his shoulder, she held him in place.

Charlie! Stevie studied her son, searching for any sign of injury or distress. He seemed impossibly small under the weight of Susan's powerful grasp. Stevie saw no bumps or bruises, no obvious signs of abuse. He stared down at the sand. She wished he would look up, even if only for a second, so she could see his eyes.

She leaned toward Dylan. "Can you hear his thoughts? Is he okay?"

"He's fine." Dylan gave a slight nod. "He's showing me that…Vanessa took care of him." He jerked his head toward Stevie, eyes wide with disbelief. "Oh no—tell me you didn't!"

The memory of her decision had flashed in her mind as soon as Vanessa appeared. Now Dylan knew what she'd been keeping from him. Stevie squared her shoulders. "I did what I had to do."

Chapter thirty

Vanessa

Vanessa took in the sight of the sprawling crowd behind Stevie. The silvery illumination of the full moon provided enough light to see many of them clearly. The Beaufort witches had come out, en masse, either to support their newly risen queen or to welcome Susan as soon as she relieved Stevie of her duties. She had no idea what the coven had told them about her mother. But she suspected that they'd been honest and shared *all* of the damning details of Susan's rapid rise to power.

The ocean wind gusted against Vanessa's back, propelling her hood forward and making it possible for her to raise her head without exposing her scars.

Charlie flinched as Susan tightened her grip on his shoulder.

"You stand right there, boy." Susan hissed in the child's ear. "Don't move. Don't use your magic. Just be still, or I'll have to kill you."

Vanessa cringed as her mother leveled her threat against Charlie.

Susan locked eyes with Stevie. "I see you brought the wit-nesses I asked for. That's good. You did as the true queen com-manded." She stood in place, never stepping out from behind Charlie. "But why do they look angry, Stevie? What lies did you tell them about me?" She laughed and gave a dismissive wave of her hand. "That's quite all right. In fact, that's why we're all here tonight. It's time for us to clear the air and set off on a new track. It's time for them to learn the truth about *you*."

Susan glanced up and then down the beach, addressing the full group. Her voice rose above the sound of the crashing waves. "If any of you are thinking you can stop me from put-ting an end to your so-called queen's reign, think again. Even combined, your power isn't enough to stop me or even hurt me. Just behave yourselves, and I will let you live."

A low rumble of murmurs erupted among the crowd. Vanessa saw the color drain from some of their faces, as though Susan's promise to let them live was not welcome news. Others stood with their jaws clenched, defiant, telegraphing their resolve to stand by Stevie.

How many of them will die tonight?

Vanessa studied the line of witches who stood alongside Stevie in the front row. She was not surprised to see the coven members standing with their queen, but the dark-haired man and woman were unexpected. Who were they? How did they intend to help Stevie?

Susan continued with her rambling speech. "You probably don't even realize that you live under tyrannical rule. Well, pre-pare to be enlightened." She held her shoulders straight. "For three hundred years, our people have lived in Beaufort. For ev-ery bit of that time, your queens and their covens have worked to hide the existence of this amulet." She raised the gold chain that hung around her neck, presenting the amethyst for the witches to view. "Why would they do that? Is it because they don't trust you? Is it because they want to keep all of its power for themselves?"

Susan released her hold on the gold chain, allowing the amethyst to fall against her chest. "I think the answer is both. Either way, it's clear that your leaders have deemed you unworthy of this knowledge." Her mouth stretched in a sanctimonious smile. "But that's not what I think. I think you're smart. I believe you deserve to know everything about the history of your own people."

An unexpected movement in the crowd caught Vanessa's eye. She spotted a middle-aged woman with short brown hair in the back row by the dunes. The woman's lips were moving, forming the same shapes with her mouth over and over again. She appeared to be chanting something, but she made no sound.

"Hiding this amulet is the least of their crimes. Did you know they kept me locked away in a psychiatric hospital for twelve years?" Susan paused for effect. "That's right. I was unlawfully imprisoned by Patricia. Did she ask any of you for permission to do that? Did she put it to a vote? No! She did whatever she wanted, just like the despot she was. It's for the best that she's gone now, don't you think?"

Vanessa's gaze fell on Stevie, who stood with her chin high and her fists clenched. She appeared poised to lunge forward at any moment, and when she did, Susan would kill her in an instant.

"But the most egregious crime was perpetrated by Stevie Lewis herself—when she attempted to *murder* my daughter. My only child." Susan placed her hand on her chest as if to

194

illustrate the heartbreak she'd never endured. "See for yourself. My Vanessa still bears the gruesome scars of Stevie's vicious attack."

Susan yanked back Vanessa's hood, revealing the full extent of her worst burns to the onlookers. A gasp rose up from the assembled witches.

The cold ocean wind scraped across the raw bald patches of her scalp. Salt spray stung the delicate, newly formed skin surrounding her deepest burns. Vanessa stood there, exposed, for what seemed like an eternity. She wanted to pull her hood back up and run away from the waking nightmare. But that wasn't an option. She could only stare into the shocked faces of the crowd, absorbing the horror reflected in their eyes. The woman in the back, who had appeared to be mouthing a chant before, stood tight-lipped now.

Vanessa waited for several long moments until she felt she had performed her duty to her mother's satisfaction. She replaced her hood and took a step back, her cheeks flushing hot with embarrassment.

"Now you know the truth of their treachery and how they've been lording it over you all of this time. You know of the hell that my poor, disfigured daughter and I have endured at their hands. So, you have a choice to make. We can start shooting each other with magic beams until you're all dead. Or, you can watch me show you what a *real* queen does." Susan looked out over the crowd. "By the time we're finished here tonight, you will all bow before me. You will grant me the gratitude and respect that I deserve!"

Everyone stared at Susan, rapt. All except for Vanessa, who now focused her unwavering gaze on Stevie.

Chapter thirty-one

Stevie

Stevie clenched her hands into tight fists while she listened to Susan's distortions of the truth. She had already come to terms with her own mortality. With her focus on protecting her people, the possibility of her ultimate sacrifice seemed a small price to pay. However, as Susan heaped falsehoods and indignities onto the memory of her dead mother, her ancestors, and her coven, something changed within her. The worry and doubt that had plagued her without mercy gave way to anger and determination.

Stay calm…and wait.

Amplified by the lingering effects of the chanted spells and the sight of her son beneath the dark witch's grasp, Stevie's magic surged within her body. Her careful plans no longer mattered, nor did her intent to sacrifice herself for her people—she stood more than ready to fight for Charlie and for all of the witches. It required every ounce of self-control she possessed just to stay in place. Instinct demanded that she rush forward and snatch Charlie away from Susan. Logic, however, insisted that she wait for a better time. She would be of no use to Charlie or her people if the dark witch struck her down now.

Charlie stared down at the sand; his golden ringlets blocked his expression from her view. Though he didn't cry out, Stevie had no doubt that he was terrified. He had to be. By now, he would have begun to detect the range of emotions surrounding him. From Susan's madness to the fear present among the assembled witches, the sheer volume of negativity surrounding him had surely taken its toll.

What would Susan do to Charlie if he interrupted her performance with a meltdown? He wouldn't be able to control himself. Would she hurt him in front of all of the witnesses?

Stevie pulled in a deep breath. She could only hope that the issue would not arise.

Susan continued to stand behind Charlie. Her smug grin showed just how much she enjoyed the attention she commanded.

"I have a big surprise for everyone." Susan clasped her hands together in an odd display of enthusiasm. She spoke with an air of showmanship that might have been comical had the circumstances not been so dire. "Watch closely. You don't want to miss a minute of this."

The amulet began to glow. Stevie watched, helpless, as the dark witch leaned in close to Charlie's ear. She tilted her head forward and willed herself to hear Susan's words above the wind and surf.

"Remember what I said, kid. Don't move!"

Susan stood up tall once again and faced the ocean, turning her back toward the crowd. If Charlie hadn't been standing in front of Susan, Stevie could have launched a surprise attack. But now, it was just too risky.

"I don't know what she's going to do. I can't hear her thoughts. She must have figured out how to block me," Dylan whispered.

Stevie had an idea of what was about to happen. Vanessa had shared her insight when they spoke on Thursday night, but even she hadn't known the full scope of Susan's plan at that point. And the sparse details Vanessa had been able to relay left Stevie with more questions than answers.

Susan raised her arms high above her head, bringing her fingertips together. In an instant, a strange shimmer appeared in the sky beyond her hands, far out over the ocean. It began to glow and brighten until it illuminated the entire beach. She lowered her arms, stretching them wide open until they fell below her hips. The glistening light expanded as it followed the guidance of Susan's outstretched arms. Finally, she drew her hands together, creating the bottom point of the traced shape.

Susan had brought an enormous oval of coruscating light into existence. It hovered in the night sky over the ocean. Stevie had no reference point with which to gauge the actual size and location of Susan's creation. There were no boats to compare it to, only open water and black sky. Urgent whispers arose from the witches on the beach, echoing Stevie's own astonishment.

A ribbon of lavender light emerged from the outer edge of the hovering shape and stretched across its center. It coasted from side to side, lengthening as it went. The pastel thread covered the width of the oval and then began to meander up and down, nearly filling it with its light. Though it never left the two-dimensional plane, it remained in constant motion.

Stevie suspected that none of the other witches had ever seen magic like this before. As her fists uncurled, she realized the show of light filled her with an unexpected tranquility. She found it impossible to look away. Excited murmurs among the witches gave way to awed silence as they too succumbed to the serene effects of the lavender hue.

A black ribbon suddenly burst into the shimmering oval. Right away, it unsettled the temporary sense of peace that Stevie felt and filled her with apprehension. Her pulse increased as it crept over and under the lavender thread, weaving its way across the space. It slithered and flowed, its stain spreading until it occupied all of the remaining area within the shape. Like its pastel counterpart, it remained in constant motion.

Buddy whined as he crouched low in front of her, his tail tucked between his legs.

Susan twirled toward the crowd, eyes bright with self-satisfaction. "This is the veil between life and death, the doorway to the afterlife."

Chatter broke out once again among the witches who stood behind Stevie. Some, she thought, sounded thrilled by this revelation. Others voiced their misgivings regarding the practice of such dangerous magic.

"All of our ancestors exist beyond this portal." Susan gestured to the shape floating over the ocean. "And only *I* can control it."

Stevie stared at the two ribbons flowing within the oval. On a level beyond conscious thought, in some primal part of her brain, she recognized what she witnessed. Good and evil. Order and chaos. She pulled her gaze away and glowered at Susan, whose pompous smirk filled her with the same sense of dread she'd experienced when the black thread first appeared.

Susan addressed the assembly of witches. "For those who are worthy, I can make it possible for you to communicate with your loved ones who have passed on." Caught up in her own conceit, she stepped out from behind Charlie and began to pace in front of the crowd.

One, two, three, four. Stevie counted Susan's steps as she moved away from Charlie. "This is my chance—it might be my only one. Be ready." She spoke in a hushed whisper, preparing Lexi and Dylan for what she was about to do.

Though neither replied, she sensed the changes in their bodies as their muscles tightened and their hearts pounded louder.

Stevie's energy burned within her. Fueled by her own outrage and boosted by the chants spoken by the witches earlier, her magic blazed hotter than ever before.

Susan continued to pace, reveling in her self-importance. Absorbed in her own show, she presented the side of herself that she wanted the witches to see. She appeared oblivious to the change in Stevie's stance.

Stevie called on the full force of her magic and directed it to her palms as Susan strode down the beach.

The dark witch pivoted and began making the return lap toward Charlie. Stevie raised her arms and fired pulses of white light from both of her hands at once, striking Susan in the chest with a fierce blast of magic. Caught off guard, Susan stumbled back, but she remained unharmed.

Without hesitation, Lexi and Dylan joined in the attack and hurled brilliant rays of light toward their target with precision. Stevie followed their assault with another one of her own.

Susan struggled to maintain her footing on the shifting sand, but she did not fall. Her expression contorted in exquisite fury. She raised her arms, providing an effective block against their magical bolts.

A flurry of sizzling lights began to streak across the beach. Every member of the coven, along with Kara and Kyle, contributed to the assault on the dark witch. Stevie heard the low hum of whispered chanting rise behind her as some of the solitary witches resumed the spell they had started before Susan's arrival.

"Power. Power. Power," they murmured in unison. Stevie hoped they were quiet enough to avoid Susan's detection.

With the help of the amulet, Susan shielded herself from most of the strikes that came her way. Now a servant to a new master, the amethyst glowed in defiance against the very people it once protected.

The blitz raged on. A few bolts of magic made it past Susan's defenses, but they had little impact on the dark witch. The coven's efforts only seemed to succeed in keeping her too busy to fire back. Stevie feared they would remain locked in the struggle until they all collapsed from exhaustion.

When that happens, Susan will kill us all.

Stevie drew upon the full force of her magic once more. It pooled in the palms of her hands, singeing her skin with its electric energy. She fired it across the sandy stretch of beach—only to watch Susan swat it away like an annoying house fly.

More bolts of force flew toward Susan, but she didn't bother to spare a glance at them as they soared her way. She stared only at Stevie now. The magic from the other coven members found their marks, and she took each hit without flinching.

Susan fell to her knees, and her glare hardened. She lifted her right arm, revealing the formidable red energy that swarmed around her hand.

The same energy that had killed Patricia.

Chapter thirty-two

Stevie

The chanting behind Stevie grew louder as more witches added their voices to the chorus. "Protection. Protection. Protection," they called in unison. No one whispered the spell now. The time for subterfuge had passed.

Stevie locked her focus on Susan. Undeterred by the chants of the crowd, the dark witch remained on her knees, and her lip curled into an arrogant sneer as she eyed her target. The red swell of malignant power surrounding her hand grew larger, crackling with electric energy, ready to hit its mark. She released it from her palm and fired her ferocious magic straight at Stevie.

The blast exploded against Stevie's ribcage, kicking her chest like an angry stallion. She flew backward, knocking down three of the solitary witches as she soared across the beach. She crashed into a dune, casting an eruption of sand several feet above her broken body.

Stevie gasped for air as her ribs collapsed on her lungs. She tried to draw in a breath but managed only to produce a gurgled rasp. She coughed, forcing the last bit of air out of her lungs. A warm, metallic liquid filled her mouth and spilled out onto her chin.

Buddy's cold nose pressed against her cheek. He let out a soft whimper before he sat down in the sand next to her head.

Urgent whispers came from all around her.

"She's over here—come quick!"

"She's bleeding!"

Unable to breathe and too weak to move, she lay in the sand. The pain seared through her entire abdomen, but she couldn't cry out.

Save Charlie! She hoped Dylan could hear her thoughts. There was nothing more she could do now. She closed her eyes and waited to die.

She began to slip away, descending into a fog of pain as the lack of oxygen began to cloud her thoughts.

"I'm here, Stevie."

It was Randy's voice; she was sure of that. She felt the gentle pressure of his hands against her sides as he employed his healing magic to stretch her crushed ribs. All at once, the bones rose up from her lungs, crackling and splintering as they moved back into place. Arrows of excruciating agony shot through her chest. She opened her mouth to scream, but she emitted no sound.

Her eyes flew open. She could only see Randy.

"Almost done, honey." He kept his voice steady though his brow furrowed with deep creases, as if he shared her agony. "Hang in there."

The holes in her lungs knitted closed, and the blood that had filled her mouth and throat dissipated. Stevie greedily inhaled as much air as she could. With each breath, she grew stronger and her dizziness lifted. Her pain subsided, allowing her thoughts to clear. She propped her elbows in the sand and tried to sit up, ready to finish her fight with Susan.

"Whoa." Randy placed his hand on her stomach. "Stay down for a minute. You can't fight yet."

"She'll come for me—and all of you." Stevie set her jaw. "I need to be ready."

Randy shook his head. "You have a little time to recover. She thinks you're dead."

Stevie eyes grew wide with surprise. She had been so lost in her own pain, she hadn't realized that her loyal coven members surrounded her. Beyond them, the solitary witches formed a deep secondary circle, obscuring Susan's view of Stevie.

"The protection spell didn't work," Stevie whispered.

"Of course it did." His hand remained on her belly, holding her in place. "A blast like that should have killed you instantly."

The full import of Randy's statement hit her. She thought of the witches who had chanted for her safety and the combined power they had brought to bear. Yet, all of that power had only been enough to allow her a few extra seconds of life following the devastating blow from Susan. She had to admit, however, that they had been precious, lifesaving seconds. They had supplied just enough time for Randy to get to her and heal her.

Susan's enraged shriek cut through the crowd of witches. "I told you only one of us was strong enough to be your queen! Do you see now what will happen if you defy me?"

The dark witch's threat rang shrill in Stevie's ears. "I need to get up now. I have to end this before anyone else gets hurt—it's me she wants."

Randy removed his hand from her stomach. "Okay, but please be careful. We need you. Now more than ever." Frowning, he helped her to her feet.

"Bring her body to me!" Susan continued her tirade from beyond the concealing group of witches. Past cajoling, past trying to win them all over to her side, her true madness was in control now. "I want to watch her carcass burn!"

Stevie's legs wobbled beneath her. She still had not regained her full strength. The witches tightened their circle around her, providing additional cover as she found her footing. They watched her, awaiting their cue.

Stevie took in a deep breath and steadied herself.

Dylan took his place on her left and Lexi joined her on her right. Their support fortified her even though she feared for their lives.

"You don't have to do this," Stevie said.

"You're our queen." Unshed tears shimmered in Lexi's eyes. "We'll stand by you through anything."

"Are you ready?" Dylan gave Stevie's hand a quick squeeze.

"I'm ready."

The throng of witches began to part, opening a narrow path for her. Stevie held her head high as she looked toward Susan, Vanessa, and Charlie still standing by the water's edge.

Charlie stared down at the sand, his hands clasped over his ears. Her stomach clenched at the sight of him. She imagined the horror he had already endured. The pain of Susan's shrieks...of believing his mother had died. *Charlie.*

Vanessa's head jerked back, and she blinked in disbelief as Stevie emerged from concealment.

Stevie stood before Susan with Lexi and Dylan at her side. The rest of her coven along with Kara and Kyle joined her as well, reforming the front line.

Wrath contorted the dark witch's features, sharpening her brow and pursing her lips. "You're still alive!" She focused her steely glare on Stevie, and a venomous grin crept across her face.

The enormous shimmering oval throbbed with life over the ocean. Stevie could only imagine what demons gathered on the other side of the veil, awaiting instruction from their master. Stevie's magic began to pool in the palms of her hands once again. She had to destroy Susan before the dark witch unleashed hell on her people.

"You can't stop me, Stevie." Susan's voice carried across the beach. "No one can." She extended both of her arms. In each hand, her vile magic surged. A fiery fury, it crackled with the volatility of its unstable owner. "But I can surely stop you!" She drew her arms back, preparing to hurl her unique brand of devastation at Stevie.

"Stop!" A woman's voice cried out.

Jolted, Stevie sought the source of the interruption.

Kara strode forward, moving closer to Susan. "Stop this. We will not let you kill our queen."

Susan threw her head back and laughed, her magic continued to swirl around her outstretched hands. She shifted her attention to Kara, eyes wide with patronizing interest. "You're not going to *let* me? Exactly how do you intend to stop me?"

Kara stared out over the ocean and flicked her wrist, a small gesture that carried an enormous impact. One by one, boats began to flicker into view. Lights from speedboats, yachts, and sailboats appeared, stretching out on either side of the veil. Some had already pulled into the shallow water just offshore.

Stevie's lips parted, and she gasped. How long had they been there?

The flotilla extended as far and wide as she could see—easily hundreds of vessels waited in the water. The closest boats were filled to capacity with witches. Stevie suspected the same held true for the ships that were too far out for her to see clearly. The Wilmington witches had come after all.

With the Beaufort witches in front of her and the Wilmington witches behind her, they had Susan surrounded.

Susan's eyebrow arched, curious but otherwise unfazed. She glanced from Kara to Stevie and back again. With a sigh, she lowered her arms, allowing the red swirl of magic to dissipate. "It's still not enough." She stepped closer to Charlie and pulled him in front of her. "Just for fun, though, let's even the playing field."

Susan turned to the shimmering oval and shouted, "Blackbeard!"

Chapter thirty-three

Stevie

A hush fell over the assembled witches, both onshore and off. All eyes remained locked on the veil that hovered above the ocean. Stevie sensed the heartbeats of those around her, ever quickening, keeping time with her own.

Near the center of the veil, a bulge appeared in the black ribbon, like a snake's belly following a feast of wharf rat. The luminescent frame pulsated as the swelling within the dark thread grew. The blackness throbbed, expanding to cover more and more of the window to the afterlife. Only a thin swath of lavender remained visible along the oval's outer edge as the bloated mass pressed forward. Stevie thought it would surely burst at any moment.

At her feet, Buddy snarled and snapped. He paced back and forth in front of her, head and tail held low. She had no doubt that he sensed the same thing she did.

Evil, pure evil.

The bulge continued to expand, growing to surreal proportion. A pointed tip poked through the swell and breached the sheen of the veil. It slid forward and revealed a long bowsprit before it sliced through the oval, setting the course for the hull that would soon follow. A massive wooden ship's bow emerged next. Gliding through with ease, it tipped down toward the water below. Stevie stared in horror as the all too familiar frigate slipped out of the afterlife and into the land of the living.

The bow continued to push onward until it dipped into the ocean. More and more of the behemoth became visible, revealing a hull and the tall masts from which its white sails hung. Finally, the ship's stern came in to view. It dropped from the shimmering oval and smacked against the ocean, pushing mammoth waves of displaced water outward. It sat deeper in the water than it should have, rocking violently at first until it settled and buoyed up to its natural floating depth.

Every resident of Beaufort knew the shape and look of the *Queen Anne's Revenge*. From the display at the Maritime Museum to countless artists' renderings, they'd all grown up with the knowledge of the vessel commanded by the pirate who had once frequented their town. Now, here it was, floating in front of them—as real and substantial as the sand beneath their feet.

Stevie had seen the *Queen Anne's Revenge* in a vision, on the night she joined the coven. Recalling the visceral fear she'd experienced at the sight of it then, she found it infinitely more imposing now.

Her mouth went dry when she spotted the flag that flapped in the wind aboard the ship. On a black background, a white skeleton held an hourglass in one hand. Its other hand gripped a spear poised above a bleeding heart. The banner served as a warning to all who encountered the ship and its infamous captain—your time has run out, and your death will be merciless.

Lexi gasped. "It can't be."

"It is." A shiver, that had nothing to do with the cold wind, raced up Stevie's spine.

The ship held steady in the water. She scanned the deck of the heavily armed vessel, where the crew scurried about and shouted—readying themselves for whatever Susan had called upon them to do. One pirate raised his cutlass into the air and yelled something that Stevie couldn't quite understand. The crew replied with enthusiastic cheers, followed by more shouting and frantic movement. She searched the deck for Blackbeard, but she couldn't find him.

"There are more coming through." Dylan pointed toward the ocean.

Stevie had been so entranced by the arrival of the *Queen Anne's Revenge*, she hadn't noticed the fleet of smaller sloops that had passed through the veil. Loaded with pirates, the boats were already advancing toward the shore. They would land on the beach within minutes.

Lexi pointed to one of the smaller vessels. "There he is!"

Stevie followed her friend's wary gaze to the lead sloop, which was closing in on the beach. On it, amid a horde of unkempt crew members, stood Blackbeard himself. A wide-brimmed hat sat atop his unruly mass of black hair. His beard, true to his moniker, covered most of his face. He wore a dark velvet jacket and sported a band stocked with curved pistols across his chest. Tucked beneath the front of his hat were long burning matches which sent menacing tendrils of smoke upward, curling in wisps around his head.

Stevie stiffened as his loathsome glare landed on her. Blackbeard seemed to know her just as she knew him. *He's coming for me.*

A panicked cry from one of the Wilmington boats yanked Stevie's attention away from Blackbeard. A woman on a yacht close to the pirate ship pointed to the starboard side of the enormous vessel. Stevie followed the direction of her pointed finger and spotted the nose of a cannon poke through a side hatch in the hull of the *Queen Anne's Revenge*.

"Jump!" The woman, along with the other passengers aboard the yacht, hit the cold ocean water in a shower of splashes and distraught cries. Stevie heard more sudden splashes as the other Wilmington witches in the line of fire followed suit and abandoned their boats.

A thunderous boom roared through the night when the cannon fired. Screams erupted among the witches, both offshore and on the beach, as the cannonball struck the now unoccupied yacht. The vessel burst into flames, igniting a maelstrom of panic. The witches in the water began a feverish swim toward the island.

A second shot erupted from the port side of the frigate, this time targeting a sailboat. The cannon spit flame as it hurled its munition. A cannonball arced forward and struck the main mast of the sailboat, snapping it in two. It missed the hull altogether and plunged into the sea. Stevie had no doubt the pirates were already reloading the weapon to make another strike. Their aim would likely improve with the next shot.

Screams, panic, chaos, cannon fire. Stevie's attention darted back to Charlie. *This must be torture for him.*

Charlie kept his hands tight against his ears as his face pinched in agony. Stevie couldn't see his eyes, but she had a clear view of Susan's bony fingers pressing into his shoulder. She gnashed her teeth.

I have to help him.

From behind Susan, Vanessa stared at Stevie—undaunted by the turmoil that surrounded her.

Stevie locked eyes with her and nodded.

Chapter thirty-four

Vanessa

Vanessa mirrored Stevie's nod, accepting the call to action that would seal her own fate. She slipped her hand into her pocket, but she hesitated as her fingers brushed against a thin piece of yarn.

There's no coming back from this. Canon fire echoed across the water and thundered through her soul.

Even though he'd clamped his hands over his ears, Charlie jumped and lurched forward at the noise.

"I told you to stay still, boy!" Susan yanked his shoulder back, forcing him to stand upright.

The intensity of Stevie's unwavering gaze bore down on Vanessa—just as it had the night she crossed the salt line.

She pulled the item out of her pocket. Glancing down at her palm, she stared at the old photo of herself and pinched the end of the black string that encircled it.

Her heart pounded as she unwound the yarn. Around and around it went, revealing more and more of the picture until only one last loop remained. Her breath caught in her throat as she gave the string a final tug and unleashed her bound magic.

It came back to her like a lightning strike. Her back arched as her body went rigid, jolted with the electric energy that had finally found its way home. Her hands sprung open on their own, releasing the string and the photograph to the wind.

Vanessa's limbs tingled, and her core burned as her power surged within her. She drove that force all the way through to the palms of her hands.

Without warning, she threw her magic around her mother's shoulders, surrounding her with a rope of charged white light. Susan released her grip on Charlie as her arms became pinned at her sides. She screeched with surprise at the unexpected attack.

Vanessa couldn't see her mother's face, but she imagined it twisting in fury. Having been the recipient of that hateful sneer more times than she could count, she had no trouble envisioning it.

Chaos erupted. Shouts and cheers rose up from the assembled witches who stood behind Stevie. Cannon fire and jeers reverberated from the swarming pirates who occupied the rapidly approaching vessels.

"Charlie, run!" Vanessa screamed as loud as she could, hoping her voice carried over the surrounding mayhem. "Run!"

The little boy took off, his hands still clasped over his ears. Though Susan squirmed, trying to free herself from the magical bonds, Vanessa held fast. But she knew it wouldn't be long before her mother gathered her wits and began to fight back.

Chapter thirty-five

Stevie

Stevie's heart soared as Charlie darted toward her. Asking for Vanessa's help had been risky, but the gamble had paid off.

He has a chance now.

"Come on, Charlie!" Lexi cheered him on. "Run!"

In spite of Vanessa's strength, Susan was far too powerful to be incapacitated for long. Stevie would have to act fast.

She leaned close to Dylan. "Grab Charlie. Keep him safe."

He took off in an instant, racing forward to rescue her son. Stevie glanced at Lexi. "Start the chants again. I'm going to need help…all the help I can get."

Before Lexi had a chance to reply, Stevie started running. Buddy scrambled to get out of her way. She heard his fervent bark, issuing a warning that she refused to heed. She drew on all of her power, both physical and magical, to sprint along the soft sand. Muscle, bone, and magic worked in harmony to propel her faster than she'd ever run before.

Stevie passed Dylan, who had already grabbed Charlie and now sped back toward the coven. She ached with an overwhelming desire to stop and hug her son, but she knew better. He was heading toward safety, and she, most definitely, was not.

Susan continued to squirm and screech from within the bonds of Vanessa's magic. She glared at Stevie and roared with palpable hatred. Even as her own flesh and blood betrayed her, her obsessive loathing remained focused on the true queen.

Stevie stared into the veil that hovered above the ocean, beyond the great pirate ship. Her feet churned through the shifting sand.

Blackness had filled most of the oval, but a sliver of lavender remained along its outer edges. Near the top of the form, the pale ribbon wiggled and began to coast down toward the center. Repeating its dance from earlier, the ribbon sought to fill the veil. Stevie pushed her legs harder and harder against the soft sand beneath her feet.

A resounding chant rose up from the assembled witches. "Power. Power. Power." Emboldened, they made no attempt to hide their efforts. They offered their power to their queen, fearless and selfless. Stevie took in their energy and combined it with her own, grateful for everything they gave her. The chanting grew even louder as the Wilmington witches picked up on it and added their own voices to the simple spell.

Stevie's power surged as the witches' song reverberated within her. Her muscles burned with effort. Energy sizzled in her veins and her bones, searing every part of her being. An agonizing euphoria. The strength of her body doubled, and her pace increased even more. She focused on the pale ribbon inside the oval, thinking of nothing else.

When her lead foot splashed into the water at the edge of the ocean, she jumped. Elevated by the sea breeze that now bent to her mighty will, she soared over the crashing waves and coasted beyond the shallows near the shore. She flew over the *Queen Anne's Revenge*, so close to its towering masts that she could almost touch them. Silence fell among the ship's crew as the wind carried her over their heads and into the heart of the veil.

Chapter thirty-six

Vanessa

Vanessa forced her arms to hold steady as she struggled to control her mother—dreading the inevitable moments to come. As soon as the shock of her betrayal wore off, Susan would break through the magical restraints.

Then I'll be punished.

With her arms pinned at her sides, Susan raged and screamed. "I'll never heal your burns! In fact, I'll make you even more hideous! You will beg for death."

Vanessa tilted her head, surprised. She hadn't expected Susan to let her live long enough to acquire more injuries. With another surge of power, she drove all of her magic down through her hands and into the binding that held her mother in place.

She couldn't see Charlie anymore—not since Dylan scooped him up and carried him into the throng of assembled witches. Wherever the boy was, she hoped that he would stay safe. *When the pirates come...* She couldn't bring herself to finish the thought.

The chants from the witches escalated to a thunderous pitch as Stevie raced toward the water's edge. They continued with even more fervor as she jumped, impossibly high, and flew into the shimmering oval above the sea.

When the queen disappeared, the witches' chanting stopped. Vanessa saw them exchange worried glances as they watched the gang of pirates make their way to the shore. Led by none other than Blackbeard himself, the crew marched onto the beach.

Vanessa gnashed her teeth and redoubled her efforts as her strength began to wane. Bolts of Susan's vile magic zipped along the restraints and snapped at her hands like taut rubber bands. She winced, knowing her mother was still too shocked to focus her power effectively. It would only get worse from here.

of time.

Blackbeard stalked toward her, followed by several long-dead members of his crew. The rest of the pirates—hundreds of them—swarmed across the beach, heading straight for the crowd of witches gathered along the sand dunes.

A tall, broad-shouldered man, Blackbeard towered over his crew. From his knee high boots to the smoke curling around his hairy face, he appeared as though he'd stepped right out of one of her school textbook drawings. Vanessa shivered. *He's far more terrifying in person.*

He strolled closer, resting one hand on his thick, leather belt. His eyes crinkled as his throaty chuckle carried on the wind.

Susan writhed and shrieked as she watched him draw near. "Kill them! Kill them all!"

Blackbeard faced his crew. "You heard the lady. Do it!" Then he looked to the dark witch who had provided his passage through the veil. "I do not recall this part of the plan, Susan." He arched a thick eyebrow and nodded toward Vanessa's magical bonds.

Susan raged against the restraints. Only her blind fury stopped her from focusing long enough to break them. "Get her off of me!"

His laugh lines disappeared as he narrowed his gaze, studying Vanessa. He tilted his head to peer beneath her hood. "You have her eyes."

Beads of sweat broke out on Vanessa's forehead as she continued to pour the full force of her magic into the bonds that she used to contain her mother. She couldn't spare the energy it would take to reply to the pirate.

"Hannah's eyes," he mumbled as he stepped closer to Vanessa. His hand shot forward in a swift lunge and grasped her throat in his long fingers.

She jerked back, stunned by his strength. Her hood dropped to her shoulders. Somehow, Vanessa resisted the urge to release Susan, even as she realized she could no longer draw air into her lungs. Blackbeard squeezed her neck harder until white spots swirled in her field of vision. She clenched her teeth against the pain and channeled her torment into her magical restraints. She held on, buying what little time she could for Charlie and the others.

Susan raged on, issuing more threats. The cannons aboard the *Queen Anne's Revenge* sounded off again. Screams came from the witches both onshore and off. The strongest witches launched a counterattack against the pirates, firing glowing bolts of power toward the unkempt men and their vessels. The battle had begun.

Her vision blurred, and Blackbeard became a dark smudge of coal between her and everything else. Jarring noises came from all around her. A cry. A yell. A boom. Overcome with dizziness, she could no longer make sense of the cacophony.

A loud pop rang in Vanessa's ears as Susan broke through her magical restraints. Blackbeard released his hold on her neck and stepped back.

Vanessa gasped and touched her hand to her throat. She filled her lungs with damp, salty air, grateful for a reprieve from the agony Blackbeard had inflicted upon her. When she finally refocused her vision, she found Susan, seething with wrath, standing before her.

Vanessa had never seen her mother so angry. Still struggling to catch her breath, she could do nothing but stand there and await her punishment.

Susan drew her arm back and flung it forward, striking her daughter across the scars and raw flesh of her burns. With an anguished cry, Vanessa dropped to her knees.

Chapter thirty-seven

Stevie

High above the ocean, the veil opened to swallow Stevie, allowing her to glide through its sheen with ease. The chanting of the witches fell away, and silence enveloped her. She floated alone in the dark, weightless, soaring through nothingness.

She couldn't see any trace of the lavender ribbon that she'd aimed for. Had she missed her target? Had she misunderstood the nature of the portal altogether?

Her forward trajectory seemed to slow, barely noticeable at first, but it soon became undeniable. She coasted a short distance and then came to a stop. Stevie blinked, hoping her eyes would adjust to reveal some hints about her surroundings.

She didn't have a second to catch her breath before she started falling. Plummeting from one point within the nothingness, she barreled through more of the same.

She had entered the veil to find her ancestors. Instead, she'd discovered only more desolation and hopelessness. There was no way out. On the other side portal, back in the land of the living, her people waited for her. They now faced Susan and the pirates without her. She had to find help, and she had to get back to them. She broke out in a cold sweat.

They need me.

"Mom!" She screamed into the depths of the void. "Mom!"

A wisp of soft silk brushed her cheek. Stevie turned her head, seeking the source of the sensation, but saw nothing. Her rapid descent through the darkness continued.

Women's voices, indistinct at first, began to surround her. They came at her from all directions. Urgent whispers and alarmed shouts echoed in the void. Stevie struggled to make sense of it.

"She needs help," cried one unfamiliar voice.

Another brush of silk came, this time across her hand.

"I just missed her!" another called with a crisp English accent.

"I've got her."

Stevie recognized that voice. She would know it anywhere. Her heart buoyed at the sound.

A tendril of silk wrapped around her arm, halting her fall. The soft fabric spread out and cradled her body. She began to rise. Her fear and uncertainty fell away, dropping into the darkness below.

She became aware of a light, coming from nowhere and everywhere at once. She rose through its lavender hue and then drifted into yet another swath of light. Awash in the golden tones reminiscent of early morning sunshine, her journey ended amid a thick mist.

Her silken cradle faded away, and her feet landed on a solid surface that lay hidden beneath the haze. Though she could not see anyone, she knew she wasn't alone.

The mist parted, revealing a multitude of eager faces. A few were familiar to her, but most she had never seen before. All were a welcome sight. One of them stepped forward, her arms outstretched.

"Mom!" Stevie ran toward Patricia and fell into her embrace, wishing she could stay there forever. But she couldn't. She had to get back to the others. With reluctance, she pulled back with tears in her eyes.

Patricia hooked her arm around Stevie's. Together, they faced the group of women who had come to greet her. The crowd stretched into the distance as far as Stevie could see. She couldn't begin to estimate the full measure of their number.

"These are our ancestors." Patricia gestured toward the vast group. "They're all the queens who came before us."

Stevie's heart pounded as she took in the sight of the assembly of women who stood in front of her. Many of them had red hair, but some were brunettes like she was. They all stood tall, wearing attire befitting the fashions of their individual generations. Some of the styles were elegant while others were simpler designs. Stevie caught glimpses of ornate gowns with full skirts as well as slim fitting, low-waisted dresses with wide, round necklines. More than one queen wore an elaborately draped toga. A plump woman with a shock of white hair atop her gray mane stepped forward. Stevie drew her hands to her mouth.

"Grandma!" Happy childhood memories flooded her mind as she wrapped her arms around her Grandmother Rose. Just like Patricia, Rose looked the same as Stevie remembered her. There were many things that Stevie wanted to share with her and even more questions she wanted to ask. It would all have to wait though. She had to get back to her people. She stepped away and addressed the assembled queens.

"I need your help."

Movement came from within the group as those who stood in the front line edged to the side, making room for someone to come forward. Two figures passed through the crowd and stepped toward Stevie.

The first one smiled as she approached. A younger woman with thick, auburn hair followed close behind. Stevie recognized them right away—Lucia and Charlotte.

"We are all ready to help you." Lucia's voice was just as clear and commanding as it had been in the vision Stevie experienced on the night of her coven initiation.

Charlotte stood with her hands on her hips. "You might recall that we have some experience with those pirates."

"You can see what's happening out there?" Stevie's eyebrows rose.

Patricia nodded. "Yes, we've watched it all unfold. This is a terrible day for our people."

"We cannot go beyond the veil. Not on our own." Lucia leaned toward Stevie as she spoke. "We need you to guide us."

Two more women raced forward, bursting through the mist—one fair, one dark. Like Charlotte, they wore corseted eighteenth century gowns, the same dresses they'd worn when they posed for the painting that now hung in Stevie's foyer.

Stevie recognized them right away. "Hannah and Catherine."

"We are not queens, but we wish to offer our assistance." Catherine dipped her head and gave a gentle smile. "If you'll have us."

Hannah, the dark-haired one, nodded in agreement. "I have some unfinished business with the pirate captain to tend to."

Stevie realized that they were watching her. All of the queens were waiting to see if she would grant the two witches passage across the veil. It wasn't a difficult decision. "Yes, of course."

"Go that way." Patricia pointed into the mist behind Stevie. "We'll follow your lead."

Stevie spun around and began to walk forward. After only a few hurried steps, the shimmer of the veil came into view. Pressing on, she led the parade of souls to the very edge of their world. She came to a stop and watched the turmoil below from her high perch within the hovering oval.

She gasped at the sight. Fighting had already begun on the island. Raised swords gleamed in the moonlight, and screams rang out as the pirates and witches engaged in battle.

She couldn't see Charlie anywhere.

Flashes of white light flew across the beach as the coven members and other skilled witches struggled to defend their weaker peers from the horde of filthy pirates that had come ashore. Someone screamed as a pistol fired, striking one of the witches in her shoulder. One of the healers who had hidden behind the dunes emerged and rushed forward to help the injured woman.

The bodies of dead and wounded pirates littered the beach. Ruth stood over one of the corpses as she fired her magic toward an oncoming group of raiders. She was holding her own—for now.

In the midst of the pandemonium, several injured witches huddled together. Alice stood in front of them, using her magic to protect them from further attack until one of the healers could get to them.

Near the sand dunes, a pirate approached one of the weaker witches from town. The young woman raised her arms in surrender, but he pressed on. He lifted his sword, fully prepared to strike her down. Another man leapt from behind a dune and tackled him, sparing the witch's life. The rescuer punched the raider over and over again until his body lay still. The man stood up and cast a quick glance up toward Stevie. *Dylan.* She watched him run toward the center of the beach, where countless more witches and pirates were embroiled in the violent clash.

Randy and one of the other healers racing toward a different cluster of fallen witches, this one guarded by Deborah. From her distant vantage point, Stevie couldn't determine the nature or severity of their injuries. She could only hope that the healers had arrived in time to save them.

The *Queen Anne's Revenge* floated below the veil, firing its cannons amid a bevy of modern vessels.

"If we jump, we'll land on the pirate ship." Stevie gestured toward it.

"I have an idea." Charlotte's brown eyes sparkled with optimism as she spoke to Hannah and Catherine. "Do you recall the spell?"

They both nodded and joined hands with the woman who had once been their queen.

Charlotte quickly explained her plan to Stevie. "I don't have the amulet this time. We could use the help of another witch."

Stevie didn't hesitate to join their magical circle. After clasping hands with Catherine and Hannah, she closed her eyes and set her intention.

"One spirit, one mind, one focus." Charlotte's voice guided them.

The four witches concentrated on their monumental task. Stevie felt their combined power swirling within the circle of their outstretched arms. Countless tiny droplets of immeasurable force formed among them and fell from the opening in the veil into the water below. Stevie visualized those magical droplets sinking all the way down to the sandy bottom of the ocean. Each one combined with, and ultimately engulfed, a grain of sand.

Their power surged between them. Stevie, Charlotte, Hannah, and Catherine all tightened their grips on one another, each using their mind's eye to call the sand into action. They pushed with all of their might, thrusting their combined torrent of energy into the sand below.

The ocean floor began to rumble. One by one, the tiny grains of sand piled up on one another. They moved slowly at first, but they soon gained momentum as billions of sandy particles dutifully obeyed the witches' commands.

Stevie visualized a gigantic sandbar rising up from the bottom of the sea and extending through the surface of the water, forcing the *Queen Anne's Revenge* above the waves.

"Well done!" Lucia clapped her hands together.

Catherine and Hannah released Stevie's hands. They, along with Charlotte, examined the results of their magical work. The sandbar they had created stretched from Cape Lookout's beach all the way up to the lower edge of the veil. The massive pirate ship teetered atop the sandy slope, lurching from side to side.

The fighting on the beach came to a swift stop. Everyone, pirates and witches alike, had paused to watch the stunning sight. Shouts of alarm came from the crew aboard the *Queen Anne's Revenge* as it wobbled on its perilous perch high above the ocean.

"Now, it's time to move the ship." Patricia shared a mischievous glance with Lucia. Together, they leaned forward, each inhaling a great breath. When they exhaled, they sent a mighty, magical wind into the vessel's sails.

The *Queen Anne's Revenge* pitched left, throwing several crew members overboard. The wooden hull groaned in protest as it tipped over and collapsed into the sea with an enormous splash. Stevie heard its thick masts snap apart as they struck the water.

Panicked cries erupted from below as the surviving members of the ship's crew fought the ocean's savage current. The few who could swim began to make their way toward the shore. Others flailed their arms in a futile attempt to stay afloat before succumbing to the pull of the sea.

"Let's go." Stevie stepped out of the veil. She marched forward, down the length of the tightly packed sandbar, leading an army of the most powerful witches the world has ever known. She guided them out of the afterlife and into a brutal war that would determine the future of their people. They continued toward the island amid shocked stares and stunned silence from the witches and pirates on the shore.

A loud voice boomed, cutting through the silence. "Keep fighting, men!"

Stevie searched for the source of the call and spotted Blackbeard standing with an irate Susan at the water's edge. He raised his cutlass above his head as he spurred his men back into action.

A roar erupted from his crew. With renewed vigor, they continued their assault on the witches. Pistols fired and swords flashed as shouts of triumph and defeat rang out from the chaos. The number of people on the beach swelled to immense proportions as more of the Wilmington witches abandoned their ships and joined the fight on the island.

Stevie descended the sandbar and stepped onto the beach. Buddy darted toward her, taking his place at her side as she faced the legion of queens who had followed her out of the veil. "Send these dead pirates back where they came from."

They all nodded and dispersed without delay. Stevie turned and began to make her way toward Susan.

"Mind if I join you?" Patricia's voice came from behind her shoulder.

"I was hoping you would." Stevie did not slow her pace.

Blackbeard stood beside the dark witch. Behind him, Vanessa struggled to bring herself to her feet. Stevie suspected that she had paid a high price for betraying her mother.

Susan's lip curled into a sneer as Stevie and Patricia approached. Blackbeard grinned as though their presence amused him. His thick, black brows rose in curious anticipation.

Patricia spoke first, addressing the pirate. "It's time for you to go back."

Blackbeard chuckled and shook his head. The ribbons tied in his beard swayed with the movement. "I'll not go willingly." He narrowed his eyes at Patricia. "As you might imagine, our accommodations in that realm are not as comfortable as yours. I find the temperature here much more agreeable."

Magic pooled in Patricia's hands. "Then I'll send you back myself!"

"I think not." Blackbeard smirked and nodded toward a group of crewmen nearby. They were on Stevie and Patricia in an instant, seizing their arms and shattering their concentration.

Buddy issued a furious growl at the attackers. He lunged forward at one of the pirates who held Stevie, sinking his teeth deep into the flesh of his leg. The pirate roared and kicked out his leg until the dog lost his hold. The man kicked again, this time striking Buddy's hindquarters.

Buddy let out a shocked yelp and limped away.

"Don't kick my dog, asshole!" Stevie yelled at the pirate.

The magic in her mother's hands faded to nothing as they both struggled to break free of their captors.

Blackbeard hurried toward his sloop.

"We have to focus." Panic singed the edges of Patricia's otherwise calm words. "We can't let him get away."

Stevie steadied her breath as she forced everything out of her mind. She ignored the pain in her arms and the screams of the embattled witches behind her. She visualized what she needed and willed it into existence. A white light suddenly blazed between them, sending the crewmen flying backward across the island.

Hannah sprinted past them. "I'll take care of Blackbeard."

Stevie knew that Hannah had the magical fortitude to stop the pirate captain. However, she chose a more physical method of subduing him. She launched herself toward his broad back and tackled him. Then she took the time to roll him over— making sure he saw her.

Hannah straddled his body and clapped her hands against both sides of his face, forcing him to look into her eyes. "Remember me?"

Winded from the unexpected assault, Blackbeard couldn't reply. A flash of light erupted from Hannah's hand. She aimed and fired, striking the center of the pirate's chest. His body dissolved into wisps of curling, black smoke. With a flick of her wrist, she sent the smoke hurling toward the veil.

The smoky remnants of countless more crew members followed as the queens of the past worked the necessary magic to send them all away. The witches finished off the remaining pirates in a matter of minutes.

Stevie stalked toward to Susan with her fists clenched. "It's your turn." She had no doubt that, by now, the dark witch had realized she was outnumbered many times over, even with the additional protection of the amethyst.

Susan stood her ground, uncompromising and arrogant. "Are you going to *murder* me here?" She nodded toward the assembled witches who, now freed from their battles, watched the confrontation unfold. "In front of all of these witnesses?"

"I'm going to take back my amulet." Stevie's expression hardened with resolution. "Whether or not you survive that process is entirely up to you."

Susan took a step back, clutching the amethyst with a fierce grip. Her frantic gaze darted across the crowd as she sought support from the masses. "There can only be one queen!"

No one cheered for her.

The dark witch scowled and lowered both of her hands as the red, raging force of her magic eddied within them.

Stevie sensed it before she heard it. Led by her mother, the queens of generations past began to chant. "Protection. Protection. Protection." Their voices stayed low and steady, producing a rhythmic whisper that did not carry above the sound of the waves crashing nearby. The witches of Beaufort and Wilmington joined the chorus. Hushed, but fierce, their intense magic surrounded Stevie.

Vanessa moved away from her mother. Stevie suspected that she had realized something that Susan, in her enraged state, could not detect.

Susan raised her arms and fired her magic with an effort so intense, she stumbled backward, almost losing her footing in the sand. The blaze of crimson energy barreled toward Stevie's chest, far more intense than the one that struck her earlier.

Stevie didn't flinch as it soared toward her. She stared straight at it and waited for the impact.

It would have killed her had it struck her. Instead, it smacked against the invisible shield constructed by the witches' chants. The shield deflected Susan's magic, bouncing it straight back to its source.

The blast sent Susan soaring down the beach, and she landed on her back near the water's edge. She lay motionless, without the slightest cry or whimper. Stevie raced toward her, fully prepared to end her life. Randy and Patricia hurried behind her.

By the time Stevie reached Susan, the dark witch's eyes were closed. Water licked the edge of her black skirt, tugging at it, urging her toward the ocean. Buddy, who no longer walked with a limp, stepped forward and sniffed her before finding his place at Stevie's side.

Randy arrived and knelt down beside Susan.

"No!" Stevie held out her arm. "Don't help her!"

Randy did not look up. "I wouldn't dream of it." He extended his hand, pressing two fingers against Susan's neck. "I just want to make sure she's dead."

Stevie stood motionless as she awaited his answer.

Randy rose to his feet, his expression devoid of emotion. "She's gone."

"It's over," Stevie whispered, more to herself than anyone else. She raised her head skyward and inhaled a great gulp of salty air. She let her lungs fill to capacity, and then with one long slow breath, she let it all out.

Patricia knelt down over Susan's body and relieved the dark witch of the amulet. She stood, cradling the amethyst pendant, and stepped toward Stevie. Her eyes twinkled with unshed tears as she stretched open the thick gold necklace and placed the chain around her daughter's neck.

The amulet fell into place, heavy against Stevie's chest. She rested her hand against the amethyst and reflected Patricia's beaming grin with one of her own.

Patricia embraced her. "I'm so proud of you." She stepped back, lowered herself to one knee, and bowed her head.

Stevie's belly fluttered with joy as she took in the sight of the hundreds, perhaps even thousands of witches now assembled on the beach. One by one, they knelt down and lowered their heads to honor her. Lucia, Charlotte, Hannah, and Catherine, along with the others who had come from beyond the veil, followed suit as did Kara and Kyle and all of the witches who had come from Wilmington. The coven members knelt down, leading the Beaufort witches in recognizing their true queen.

Beyond them, a lone figure stood by the surf. Whatever Vanessa had endured at Susan's hands, the dark witch had been her mother. Stevie could see the pain that lingered in her eyes. In spite of it all, Vanessa dropped down to one knee and bowed her head. Her hood fell forward, concealing her scarred face.

Chapter thirty-eight

Stevie

Patricia rose to her feet and the others did the same. They had a great deal of work to do, so no one wasted a moment getting to it. There were boats to repair and witches to heal. Though the pirates had all returned to their place beyond the veil, their ships remained. That, too, would have to be dealt with.

Before Stevie could focus on anything else, she had to find Charlie. She needed to hold him. She wanted to tell him that everything was going to be all right. She could say that now, at last, because she knew it was true. She scanned the crowd in search of her son, but she didn't see him.

Dylan caught her eye. "I'll get him." He ran off toward the sand dunes.

The queens of the past worked shoulder to shoulder with the witches of the present to clear the disarray that littered the once pristine island. Amid the sea of well-worn blue jeans, wide skirts and petticoats stood out.

The undyed woolen togas of the queens who had lived in ancient Rome fluttered in the ocean breeze as their copious golden jewelry sparkled in the moonlight. They worked together with some of the Wilmington witches to repair the modern boats damaged by cannon fire. Another small group, led by a queen who wore a frilly white blouse atop a long, bell-shaped skirt, scanned the water in search of any remaining evidence of drowned pirates.

Lucia, Charlotte, Hannah, and Catherine stood at the water's edge studying the sloops that had accompanied the *Queen Anne's Revenge*. After a brief discussion, they each raised their arms and directed their combined magic toward the boats. One by one, the sloops dissolved into wisps of black smoke. The witches dispatched them to the veil with ease.

They focused their attention on the sinking monstrosity that was Blackbeard's flagship. The *Queen Anne's Revenge* lay on its side, groaning under the enormous pressure of the water it was taking in. With each passing second, it slipped further below the surface. Blackbeard's banner, which had warned of a cruel and merciless death, floated limp on the tide. Its once threatening skeleton now lay impotent. Lucia, Charlotte, Hannah, and Catherine combined their power and fired a bold ray of light at the vessel. It didn't give up its hold on the world quite as readily as the sloops had, so they pressed on, focusing their considerable might to destroy it.

A symphony of cracks and pops emerged from the vessel. Thick wooden boards snapped and the great ship crinkled as though it were little more than a thin sheet of paper. It collapsed in a giant cloud of black smoke, which they waved toward the veil with synchronized flicks of their wrists.

Just one remnant of the night's evil lingered—Susan's body. Vanessa sat beside it in solitary vigil. Stevie stepped toward her, unsure of what to say. She only knew that was where she needed to be. Drawing closer, she noticed that Vanessa shed no tears, but her anguished expression betrayed the emotion that roiled within her. Stevie waited beside her in silence.

Vanessa glanced up and met Stevie's gaze. "We had a complicated relationship."

Of that, Stevie had no doubt. "We're going to have to take her soon. We'll give her a burial at sea." She spoke softly, conscious of the fact that her victory had meant a loss for Vanessa.

And we couldn't have done it without her.

"Come with me." She extended her hand to help her former adversary to her feet.

Vanessa complied without a word. As she stood, she adjusted her hood and hung her head to hide her scars. She followed Stevie through the crowd of mingling queens and witches.

Stevie searched the group for Randy. The healers had already treated the most serious injuries. Now, they focused on mending scrapes and sprains, making quick work of the process. The witches of Beaufort and Wilmington would all be made whole soon.

She spotted the elderly doctor as he directed one of the other healers to an injured witch near the sand dunes. She didn't know how Randy would react to the request she was about to make, but that wouldn't stop her from making it. He eyed her with a cheerful grin, leading her to suspect that he already knew what she wanted.

Stevie faced Randy with Vanessa at her side. "Will you help her?"

Randy glanced from Stevie to Vanessa and back again, his blue eyes sparkling. "It would be my pleasure." He reached forward and pulled Vanessa's hood away from her face.

"I have others." Vanessa unzipped her hoodie and pulled it off of her shoulder, revealing similar scars along her left arm.

Randy placed his hand on Vanessa's arm, and she winced at his touch. "This won't take long." Even as he spoke, the burns began to fade. Red turned to pink and pink faded to her flesh tone. Then he raised his hands and cupped her face. Stevie watched the rippled scar tissue smooth in response to his healing magic. The burns faded away just as they had on her arm, revealing a youthful, even complexion. Randy adjusted his hands, lifting them to encompass Vanessa's battered scalp. Her black hair began to grow, filling the bald patches and extending down her shoulders, once again becoming a glorious, shiny mane.

Satisfied with his work, Randy lowered his hands and stepped back. "There. All better now."

Vanessa touched her cheek. She stroked its smooth surface in disbelief. "It doesn't hurt anymore..." Eyes wide, she stared at Stevie and Randy. "I...I don't know how to thank you."

Stevie waved away her comment. "No thanks needed. You helped us—we're happy to help you."

Vanessa's lip twitched with a hint of a smile before she walked away from Randy and Stevie.

Randy watched Vanessa's retreating frame. "Hell of a risk you took. But I guess it paid off."

Stevie blinked, recalling the initial surprise she'd experienced when Vanessa had crossed the salt line and entered her house that night. "It was her idea to wait until tonight to unbind her powers. She was concerned that Susan would detect her magic if she did it any sooner."

Randy just shook his head and left in search of patients to mend.

With the cleanup work completed, Stevie noticed that many of the queens had already begun to ascend the sandbar, heading back to their home beyond the veil. The Wilmington witches, as well, had started to board to their boats. The crowd on the beach thinned at a rapid pace. She searched the remaining faces for her mother.

Kara approached her. "We're all going back to Wilmington now. We'll take Susan's body with us and drop it far off the coast so there's no chance of it washing ashore." Her shoulders relaxed, and her eyes crinkled as she grinned. "I'm glad you called for us." She extended her arm, offering a handshake.

Stevie accepted her hand. "Thank you for answering the call."

Kara glanced to the fleet of vessels she'd brought with her. "I think it's a good thing that our groups have united. We're stronger together."

"I agree." Stevie smiled, almost bursting with joy, as Kara walked away. She took in the sight of the two distinct tribes now joined as one people. *My people.*

In the distance, she caught Lexi and Kyle in the throes of a passionate goodbye kiss. She shook her head and chuckled. She'd had no idea that the two had grown so close. Then again, it was Lexi, and Stevie knew better than to be surprised by anything her best friend did when it came to romantic relationships. She had a feeling that she'd be seeing Kyle around Beaufort a lot in the coming days.

She found Patricia engaged in lively conversation with Deborah. They laughed together, just like old times. Stevie stepped toward them, hesitant, unwilling to break up the reunion of the two lifelong friends. Deborah noticed her and waved her forward, so Stevie continued on until she met up with her mother.

Patricia gave her a tender smile. "I'm afraid I have to go now." She nodded toward the veil. Stevie followed her gesture to see that most of the queens had already left the beach and were now walking up the sandbar in a parade of high held chins and antique fashions.

"Please stay, Mom." Stevie's voice cracked. "I miss you."

"My time here is done. We both know that." Patricia rested her hand on Stevie's shoulder. "But we also know that we'll meet again, don't we?"

Stevie's lip quivered as she nodded. Her mother enveloped her in one final embrace.

"Look after your father for me." She pulled away from Stevie and gripped her hands in a final supportive squeeze. "Till we meet again." Saying nothing more, she began to make her way to the sandbar.

The last of the Beaufort witches left the beach, heading toward the walkway that would take them to the sound side of the island, where their boats waited. Stevie watched the flotilla move away from the shore as the Wilmington witches began their journey home with Susan's body onboard one of the yachts. All that remained now were her coven members and Vanessa.

Stevie yawned and glanced at her watch while Buddy stood beside her with his tail wagging, ever faithful. She raised her head up to view the full face of the moon, which hung high in the late night sky. She slipped her hand down and plucked the piece of sea glass from her pocket. She had almost forgotten that she'd brought it with her. As she rubbed her hand across its matte surface, she wondered if it had helped her.

She thought of her impossible flight into the veil, buoyed by the air and carried by the wind. She remembered drawing the sandbar up from the earth, creating a pathway. And she considered the water itself, which had swallowed the *Queen Anne's Revenge* and so many of its vile crew. Fire, at least in the traditional sense, had not been present for the battle. However, she knew a blaze burned within her—hotter now than ever before.

Stevie looked to the sandbar, where her mother followed Lucia and Rose as they neared the veil. One by one, they disappeared behind its shimmering glow. "Goodbye, Mom," she whispered as Patricia slipped out of sight.

The sandbar began to crumble. Chunks of hard packed sand plummeted into the ocean and splashed through the surface. Individual granules rained down from its tall sides, sinking until they reached their home at the silty bottom of the sea. The deconstruction continued until the sandbar dissolved completely, bringing forward the tide as it displaced the water just offshore.

Stevie faced the enormous hovering oval. She paused for a moment to watch the black and lavender ribbons nestled among each other, marveling at the intricacy of their design.

Time to shut this door.

She cupped the amethyst that now rested against her chest until the amulet showed her the silent spell she needed to close the veil. Its power mingled with her own, and she raised her arms high above her head, mentally calling for the mystical portal to close. She brought her hands together with a clap and then lowered them, mimicking the oval shape. The veil folded in on itself, sealing away the angels and demons within its mist.

"Stevie!" Dylan called from some distance behind her.

She whirled around and found him walking in her direction, holding Charlie by the hand. Her heart leapt to her throat.

"Charlie!" She raced toward him, sending sand flying out behind her feet. The little boy let go of Dylan's hand and ran toward her as well. They met in the middle of the beach. She fell to her knees and opened her arms, enveloping him in her embrace. They clung together for several moments.

Stevie raised her head and met Dylan's gaze, knowing now that he had carried her son far into the dunes to hide him from Susan. "Thank you," she mouthed.

She nestled her face in Charlie's golden curls. When she pulled back, she looked him up and down, seeking any sign of injury. "Are you okay?"

Charlie nodded. He gave her hair a quick tousle and then leaned in to plant a kiss on her forehead. "I love you."

Stevie couldn't breathe. The sound of his voice caused her heart to thunder so hard she feared it might explode. She wrapped her son in her arms again. "I love you too, Charlie."

epilogue

Stevie

Stevie watched the sunset from her porch. A full week had passed since the confrontation with Susan, and life had already returned to normal in Beaufort. Well, as normal as it could get for a secret group of witches.

Charlie had gone back to school, thriving in the supportive environment provided by his teacher, Maura. Reconstruction had begun at Coastal Visions, and they had a grand reopening date set for early December, just in time for the Christmas rush. The coven had already resumed its more mundane role of operating the Beaufort Historical Society—with Stevie at the helm.

Buddy lay at her feet on the wooden boards of the porch. Perpetually happy now that the threat against his new owner had been resolved, he thumped his tail against the boards. Stevie had set up a dog bed along with food and water for him inside the house, but he preferred the porch most days. He'd become part of the family, faithful as though he had been with them forever. Stevie leaned over and scratched his head.

She yawned as the last golden rays of the setting sun disappeared beneath the horizon. Exhaustion had haunted her all week—not surprising given the immense outpouring of magical effort required to bring down Susan. Since Charlie was with his father for the weekend, she expected to have plenty of time to catch up on sleep.

The thought of her son brought a smile to her lips. Charlie was changing, growing, and maturing. Stevie had no doubt that more challenges would come as he moved through his childhood, but she also understood that he had a good chance of having a fulfilling life.

She'd always had a spark of hope for him, but for the most part, relentless anxiety had consumed her. Worry for his well-being and for his future had been a constant in her life. Now, for the first time since his autism diagnosis, hope outweighed the gnawing fear in Stevie's heart.

Her front door opened and Dylan emerged from the house. She greeted him with a smile and a kiss.

"Want to go for a walk?" He tugged on her hand.

"Sure."

They descended the porch steps together, and she felt the gentle touch of his hand on the small of her back. "Let's go over here." He nudged her across the street and onto her dock.

She walked beside him without saying a word. It was a lovely night to be on the water.

He smiled and took her hand, guiding her toward the far end. White votive candles appeared and illuminated spontaneously with each new step they took. One by one, to their right and to their left, the candles lit up to greet them as they proceeded. When Stevie and Dylan reached the square platform at the end of the dock, the candlelight encircled them, flickering in the cool, salty breeze.

"Stevie Lewis." Dylan lowered himself to one knee without breaking eye contact with her. "My queen." He pulled a rounded jewelry box from his pocket and opened it, revealing a ring nestled in velvet.

Her stunned gaze fell on the iridescent face of the moonstone cast in a simple gold setting. Dylan could have selected any jewel, of any size, to present to her in this moment, but she knew he'd chosen this one to honor her, for all that she was and all that she would be. She pressed her hand against her chest and bit her lip.

"Will you marry me?"

Butterflies took flight in her stomach as she envisioned their future together. "Yes."

Stevie tried to wrap up her first meeting as the official president of the Beaufort Historical Society. They had discussed, ad nauseam, the details of the upcoming holiday bake sale—settling the when, where, how, and why of the event. All she had left to do was bring the meeting to a merciful end. Only then could she finally enjoy that nap she'd wanted to take since she'd opened her eyes that morning.

"Okay, well, I think we've covered everything." Stevie stifled a yawn.

Alice raised her hand suddenly. "I move that we go forward with establishing a school for young witches."

And with that, the meeting of the Beaufort Historical Society changed into a coven meeting. Stevie remained silent as she awaited the replies of her coven members.

"I second the motion." Dylan raised his hand and winked at Alice in solidarity.

Stevie rested her hand on the table, and the gold band of her engagement ring clinked against the tile top. She smiled at the sound. "All right then. All in favor say "aye.""

Ruth, Randy, Deborah, and Lexi agreed without further discussion. The plans for the school would move forward. No young witch would ever doubt her place in this world.

"Very well then, let's go ahead with the plan to start a school for young witches here in Beaufort. If there's nothing else..." She glanced around the table, seeking any signs of potential interruption from the coven members. Seeing none, she breathed a sigh of relief. "Meeting adjourned." She thanked them for their time.

Everyone stood up from the table except for Deborah, who continued her fervent knitting on her current project. Stevie watched the witch's hands move with ease, shifting her needles amid the pink yarn she had chosen for what appeared to be a new blanket. *Pink—the color of health.*

Stevie pointed to the pastel yarn. "Is someone sick?"

Deborah looked up from her work with a twinkle in her eye. "Oh, no. Not at all." She stuffed the half-finished blanket along with her needles into her canvas tote and rose from her seat at the table.

Stevie walked all of them to the foyer, where she accepted their well wishes for her engagement, and then she ushered them out of her house.

Dylan stroked her arm as he reached her front door. "Do you mind if I go with Alice to search for locations for our new school?"

"Go ahead." Stevie wanted nothing more than a nap and a giant slice of pizza, so a little alone time suited her just fine. "Let me know what you find."

With the coven gone and Charlie away with his dad, she had the house to herself. Even Buddy had wandered off, having left for some grand adventure only stray dogs could appreciate.

Stevie plodded into her den, heading straight for the comfort of her couch. She sat down on it, ready to fall over, when an unexpected knock on the front door echoed through the house. She rose to her feet, shoulders slumped, and walked across the house back to her foyer.

Stevie forced herself to present a welcoming façade and then opened her door to find Vanessa standing on her porch. Impossibly tight, Vanessa's tank dress clung to her curves. Her crown of wavy, black hair cascaded over her shoulders and down her back. Stevie had not seen her since the night at the Cape. The difference was stunning. Though Randy had restored Vanessa's appearance to its original state, Stevie knew that the witch's heart had been forever changed.

"Hey." Her voice sounded sultry once again, and she stood with an air of newfound confidence. "I just wanted to say goodbye to Charlie. I wanted to thank him for making me a better person."

"I'm sorry, but Charlie isn't home right now. I know he'd love to see you though. Can you come back tomorrow afternoon?"

Vanessa shook her head. "My flight leaves tonight. I'm going back to Los Angeles for a while, for a few weeks anyway. I have some loose ends to tie up."

"Charlie will be sorry that he missed you," Stevie said. "I'll be sure to tell him that you stopped by."

"I'd like to come back." Vanessa met her gaze. "To Beaufort, I mean. I want to *live* here."

Stevie stood still for a long moment, thinking. As she stared into Vanessa's emerald eyes, she realized the witch was asking permission from her queen to stay in Beaufort.

She sensed the mutual forgiveness that stretched between them. Somewhere beneath that bridge lay all of the mortal and psychic pain the two had caused each other. Just out of view, but not forgotten.

She faced her one-time nemesis. She'd already come to a decision, and it had been an easy one. "You're welcome to come back to Beaufort if you want. I could use your help with the, uh, Historical Society, if you have the time to spare."

Vanessa's expression lit up with relief, and her full lips stretched into a cheerful grin. "It would be my pleasure."

"Stop by when you get back into town. There will be a place for you at my table."

Vanessa's smile faltered. "Will the others be comfortable with me?"

"They all saw what you did that night. They know the risk you took—and what you sacrificed. Like it or not, you're one of us now."

Vanessa nodded. She turned to leave, but stopped to face Stevie once again. "I think it's really cool that Charlie has the ability to make everyone love him."

"That's not magic. That's just Charlie."

When Vanessa left, Stevie ambled back to her den and sank into the comfort of her couch. She closed her eyes and pushed away the nagging thoughts about the Historic Society's upcoming bake sale. She lay there, listening to the steady thrum of her own heartbeat—a simple comfort, steady and reliable. Her breaths came deep and easy.

Stevie's eyes suddenly sprung open. She heard something more than her own pulse in the stillness of the old house. A steady pitter-patter made itself known. Soft and delicate, it would have been easy to miss.

Her overwhelming exhaustion. Those endless cravings for pizza. She'd been through this before...when she was pregnant with Charlie.

A tiny, second heartbeat throbbed within her. She had no doubt of it now. She listened to it, marveling at its music.

Her mind raced with memories. Seeing now the clues that she'd missed in the craziness of the last couple of weeks.

There has always been a girl child to succeed the queen.

She recalled Deborah's work on the new pink blanket, even though no one was sick.

She thought of Randy's hand on her stomach the night of the battle. At the time, she'd assumed he had been holding her down to keep her from going back to the fight too soon. But that wasn't what he'd been doing at all. He had been healing her baby!

Stevie heaved herself up from the couch, stunned. The elder witches had figured it out before she had.

The delicate heartbeat pulsed quicker than her own. There had been a time when the thought of another child would have filled her with fear. Now, there was only hope. Hope for a bright future for both of her children. Hope for long lasting peace for her people.

All of her doubts fell away. Stevie rested her hands on her belly as a slow, steady smile stretched across her face.

"My daughter, your kingdom awaits."

the end

About the Author

Chrissy Lessey is a beach bum with a deep appreciation for good jokes, strong coffee, and salt air. She lives on the beautiful Crystal Coast of North Carolina where she finds endless opportunities to procrastinate and daydream. A long-time fan of rock music, Chrissy married a talented drummer. She still loves listening to him play—as long as it's not in the house. Together, they have two energetic children and an ill-mannered dog.

She enjoys connecting with her fans both in person and online. Visit ChrissyLessey.com or follow her on Facebook, Twitter, and Instagram to stay up-to-date on her latest book news and upcoming appearances.

acknowledgements

The Crystal Coast Series would not have been possible without the support of my family. They suffered through six long years of my writing, revising, editing, re-writing, re-revising, and re-editing without (too much) complaining. Jeff, Jacob, and Sarah—I'm grateful for your patience!

Special thanks to Erin and Deek at Tenacious Books Publishing. It's been fun accomplishing the impossible with you.

I'm fortunate to have a stellar editorial team to work with. Chris Alderson, Erin Rhew, and Cristen Iris—I appreciate your expert advice. Thanks to my beta readers and proofreaders—Missy Barber, Nicole Collins, Peggy Sue Dupuis, and Heather Waterman—for bravely diving into my unpolished manuscripts and sharing your insight with me. Bonus points to all of you for not laughing at those early drafts.

I've had the great pleasure of connecting with local fans at Crystal Coast Con—Eastern North Carolina's Premier Sci-Fi and Fantasy Convention. Many thanks to Connie Nolter, mastermind of this incredible event, for including me, and to Tracy Gillikin for her exceptional hospitality.

Much appreciation to Craig Morton of Sight Photography for creating the trailer for The Crystal Coast Series.

While working on this series, I occasionally encountered topics that required more information than I could glean from the internet. Thanks to Patrick Langdale of Captain Patrick's Crystal Coast Waterway Tours, Jessica Calla, and Dango Nguyen for allowing me to pester you with questions.

For my friends and fans—and the fans who became friends—I'm grateful for your support and enthusiasm. Thanks for reading, reviewing, and recommending my books!

praise for the crystal coast series

"*The Coven* is atmospheric, intriguing, and at times deeply moving. With terrific characters, a vivid setting, and plot that clips along smartly, this book is a great read. A series to dive into!"

-Paula Brackston, *New York Times* Bestselling Author of *The Witch's Daughter*

"Very well-written, easy to read and engaging. I was surprised by how much I cared about the characters. For me, this demonstrates Lessey's ability to cross genre boundaries and engage ALL readers."

-Steph Post, author of *Lightwood*

"Lessey's story is both heartwarming and surprisingly believable."

-C.H. Armstrong, author of *The Edge of Nowhere*

"I devoured this book in one sitting! *The Coven* **opens the reader's mind to the magic all around us. Ms. Lessey's beautiful account of the lengths a mother will go to for her child is splattered with a family's age-old quest for revenge, a touch of romance, and a loving account of a small town community's bond and commitment to each other. Fans of Nora Roberts' light paranormal stories (Cousins O'Dwyer Trilogy, Three Sisters Island Trilogy) will lov***e The Coven.***"

-Jessica Calla, author of The Sheridan Hall Series and *The Love Square*

"It's *Practical Magic* **meets** *Steel Magnolias***."**

-Chanda Platania, Neuse Regional Library

"The Coven is extraordinary for two reasons. First, it is a well-written story with fully developed characters. The story draws you in and doesn't let go. The second reason I love *The Coven* is the way the author treats her autistic character. Too often, these depictions wind up being caricatures of autism. Chrissy Lessey manages to avoid this by presenting a realistic character who is multifaceted and engaging. My heartfelt thanks for that."

-Josh Leone, author of The Calling Tower Saga

"Chrissy Lessey doesn't disappoint with her fast-paced, easy-to-read, enjoyable witch story. I loved the setting and the relationship between Stevie and her son Charlie, who has autism. The connection of the witches to the famous pirate Blackbeard is a great twist."

-Teri Harman, author of The Moonlight Trilogy

www.ingramcontent.com/pod-product-compliance
Lightning Source LLC
Chambersburg PA
CBHW021006120726
47905CB00009B/2885